The Fallen

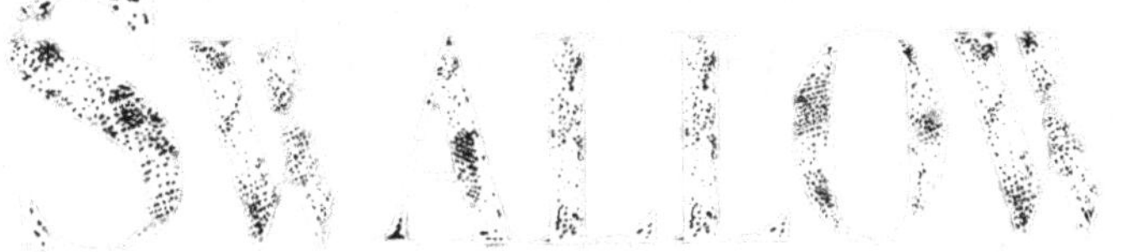

Book One

Contents

Prologue:
The Norn's Prophecy

From the frigid north, a howling wind swept across the desolate and barren landscape, unleashing its fury on the land below.

Heavy clouds rolled and churned across the sky while bolts of lightning streaked through the heavens, followed by the deafening rumble of thunder passing through the air.

Amidst this tempest, three old and haggard women danced manically around a majestic tree. They were in a trance, their eyes white, their bodies vibrating violently of their own volition. The three chanting in strange tongues, their loud hums reverberated across the otherwise barren land.

As lightning flashed once more and a clap of thunder roared, a sudden calmness spread across the midnight sky. The hauntingly melodious echoes of the women's voices fell into a deafening silence; it lasted but a few moments, after which one of the three women spoke up, her words only just audible through the wind. "A son will ascend from the caves of darkness!" she began. "Feared above all else, he will rule the realms. Hark! No soul that lives can defeat him. But a daughter, born on the equinox solstice betwixt the twin moons, shall be his downfall! Beware, for the dark prince shall not be vanquished until her deathly shadow is cast."

As the women began to chant again, the majestic tree writhed and contorted in pain as if being tortured. Their words travelled through the land, forests, and woods, reaching into every heart.

Chapter One
The Scourge of Mercia

He was dying. The man crawled helplessly along the wet, marshy, and uneven ground, leaving a trail of blood behind over the rocks and the grass, pools of red wetness soaking the barren earth.

Over the top of him, a tall, wiry, masked man in a red cape loomed.

Waving his wand, the attacker conjured an electric bolt that struck the man as if he had not already taken enough of a beating. Writhing and flailing on the ground, the victim released an ear-shattering scream. Feebly, he attempted to raise his own wand to ward off the inevitable, but the masked figure was moving with agile speed. Swift and brutal, the figure delivered yet another vicious strike, this time a kick, sending the wand flying free of the victim's bruised grasp.

With all his weight, the attacker shoved his boot down onto the defeated man's hand, grinding it down into the stony earth as hard as he could while the victim screamed, trying to pull away.

Utterly helpless, the man's shrieks were visceral; he failed to escape the boot's grip.

With a single swift wave of the masked attacker's wand, a sudden burst of electric energy crackled and surged, now striking down upon the man's bloodied and bluish bruised back.

A heart-rending wail rose high, followed by silence. He was dead.

As the masked figure stood looming over the prostrate

body, a subtle change in the air caught his attention; he turned his gaze towards an outhouse nearby, almost as if sensing something.

But just as suddenly as the feeling had arisen, it dissipated into nothingness.

Undeterred, the masked figure muttered a few incantations, then vanished too.

***

The teenage boy stood peering through the tiniest crevice in the outhouse wall, his blood running cold, making him tremble as he caught sight of Selwyn's lifeless body sprawled on the ground.

Selwyn had been like a father to him. Because of this, the teenager longed to run to his side and hold him, but he knew that doing so would only lead to his own death at the raiders' hands.

He could almost hear Selwyn's voice replaying, imploring him, "Protect yourself!"

After a moment, the teen boy inhaled a deep breath and peered through another narrow crevice on the opposite side of the outhouse. There, he caught sight of Racelyn, the village wand maker, frantically trying to escape his burning shop, the pungent and acrid smoke billowing freely from its small doorway. His hair and clothes were singed, his eyes were red, and his face was streaked with soot. He stumbled and fell as he made his way out, and the teenage boy could see the desperation in his eyes as he tried to get up and continue running.

A searing, electrifying surge erupted and struck Racelyn, killing him instantly. As he stared at the dead forms of his fellow villagers scattered over the ground, the teenage boy cried. This scene was a stark reminder of the raiders' savage and merciless deeds.

The village descended into turmoil, its air thick with the acrid stench of black smoke still pouring free from all the voracious fires, twisting and dancing high above the houses.

Beads of sweat formed on the teenager's brow from the blistering heat. In this tumult, the resounding echoes of splintering wood and crumbling masonry filled his ears, mingling with the harrowing cries of the dying. The once majestic Mercia Wizardry Ministry, sitting proudly at the top of the hill like a beacon of hope and magic, was now also burning fiercely. The inferno cast an eerie deep red glow over the chaos, illuminating the night sky in a hellish hue, daubing it.

His eyes widened with terror, his gaze fixating on yet more raiders marching down the hill towards the outhouse and village, their fearsome wands gleaming in the flickering firelight.

Dread and terror converged, seizing him in their grip, rendering him motionless as if bound by a pair of invisible shackles.

He did not dare move, not an inch, in case the same should happen to him. Within this paralysing tumult, a desperate cry issued forth from his lungs regardless.

It was a yearning plea for sanctuary, an escape from the overwhelming waves of emotion.

His legs gave way, and he fell, the solid ground welcoming him like some fond old friend.

He found himself sitting on the cold surface for what seemed like an eternity, staring off into space, just trying to gather his wits together again. In time, he managed to compose himself enough to begin looking around, considering his options. Then, his eyes grew wide as he whispered to himself, "Olesia." He began trembling with the realisation.

He had been standing here a long time, peeking through the spy holes in the outhouse wall, oblivious to the world he had just left behind.

Had he really forgotten about his three-year-old sister? He now fervently hoped that she was under the protection of Annis, Selwyn's wife, one of their trusted guardians.

He rose with caution, moving as quietly and stealthily as possible within the confined space.

Taking a deep breath to calm his racing heart, and suppressing the nausea roiling in his guts, he slowly opened the door of the outhouse.

Its rusty hinges groaned, sending a shiver down his spine.

He turned around again, intent on seeing what else had occurred outside before daring to exit. His eyes widened as he peered into the gloom, spying through one of his peepholes.

He looked left, then right. *Hush …*

His heart thumped within his chest, seeing that nearby, a group of raiders had gathered.

Drawing upon all his bravery, he bolted from the outhouse, managing to sneak past the amassing raiders undetected. He found refuge behind a cluster of vast barrels pushed outside by the local tavern, each one empty and awaiting collection.

There, this teen boy crouched, waiting until the coast

became clear.

The more time passed, the more the adrenaline coursing through his veins began to subside, replaced by a gnawing fear that clung to him. A sudden gust of wind carried in his direction, the distant cries of the wounded and the scent of smoke intertwined, creating a symphony of anguish that clawed at his resolve. Now, he was wishing he had never moved from the outhouse.

Here, the night was pungent with the smell of burning and pierced by noises of unsettled talk.

Tall flames from the many crackling structures painted a grim tableau of destruction, illuminating the desperation etched across his dirt-streaked face. He knew that mere moments of respite behind these barrels—as solid and tall as they may be—would not suffice; every heartbeat seemed to count down the time until the raiders' insidious gaze would once again sweep over the hidden corners of the village. And he would be found in one, hiding, like the rest.

His breath hitched as he peeked around cautiously, surveying the area.

There is no one, he thought. *It's safe enough. Time to make a move.*

With trepidation, he rose from his hiding place, his eyes darting frantically, searching for any signs of movement aside from his own, any indication that the raiders had homed in on his trail.

No, still nothing. But I swear, a half-deaf man on the other side of the village could hear my pathetic heart beating like this! Hush, my heart ... you will give away my location ...

He darted out like a rodent from his narrow, cramped hiding spot, sprinting past scattered bodies, each a grotesque display of mangled limbs, glassy eyes and oozing wounds.

The air hung heavily with the metallic scent of blood, the same iron-rich odour to be found down by the metal forge—only right here, it would be rich with crimson and many hues.

He was glad of the night's cover to conceal the many colours of death, that much was certain.

But he had to walk tentatively since the ground beneath his feet felt slippery with the congealing aftermath. His laced boots with their leather soles slipped and slid this way and that.

Now and then, he stumbled on something, almost tripping, grabbing at the corner of a house or a stony wall to keep him upright among the many projections reaching up to make him fall.

Limbs. Yes, these were stiffened arms and legs, maybe heads too, but mostly limbs contorted at unnatural angles, and a little farther along, a face contorted in another grimace of sheer agony.

Rushing through the nightmarish scene, he briefly glanced at the shattered figures around, his stomach churning, a bitter taste lingering in his mouth as he forced himself to look away.

Carnage, this was, absolute hell on earth.

The broken and bloody bodies blurred together, and he struggled to shake off the gruesome images, each one becoming imprinted in his mind.

He told himself, *it's not a body! It's just my imagination, playing tricks!*

But the staring glazed eyes and disgusting, overpowering stink gave away the truth of things.

A visceral reality clawed at his senses, threatening to

overwhelm him with fear and revulsion. The bodies were already beginning to decay, and now and then, a buzzing sound smacked into his ear, a fat fly on its way to fill yet another carcass with wriggling maggots. The ground near the deaths was growing increasingly slick with the slippery fats, the oozing, suppurating, fetid juices of many human torsos, leaking all their insides as they quickly turned to putrefaction.

The desperation to flee from the horror fuelled his every stride, the urgency intensifying with each passing second. He wanted to vomit and to scream.

But he could do none of these because of the need for quickness and stealth.

Ragged gasps and a cold sweat clung to his brow as he pressed on, propelled by the instinct to survive this unholy, unimaginably horrible nightmare.

Among the chaos of broken bodies and spilled blood, the teen grappled with an overwhelming sense of vulnerability. These shattered forms … They all could have been friends, neighbours, or even strangers, but they were all just like him; this awareness deepened his sense of helplessness, a stark reminder of the indiscriminate brutality that had befallen those he might have known.

The thickest black smoke filled the air now, making it difficult to breathe.

He tried his best not to cough and draw attention to himself, but the smoke was clawing at his throat by now, making it nearly impossible. He clenched his fists and then loosened them, and thought, *how am I supposed to save her?* Then, he remembered something. *Selwyn.*

Yes, Selwyn was responsible for finding and destroying dark and dangerous magical objects on behalf of the Mercia

Wizardry Ministry. Selwyn had to dispose of the whole lot!

But this boy knew something else, too; he knew that Selwyn tended to keep hold of some of the magical items secretly, purportedly in the hopes of understanding them better at a later date.

Selwyn's transporter device, a powerful magical artefact resembling a wooden recorder, sprang to mind. Though it appeared to be nothing more than a simple flute-like instrument, it was imbued with capricious and unpredictable magic. Selwyn had repeatedly warned him of its erratic nature, urging caution and emphasising its use only in the most dire of emergencies. "It's not a toy, you understand, boy? Not a toy."

Remembering the man's voice made him shudder; around Selwyn, he always felt as if he was in trouble even when they were just having a normal conversation. For sure, he could be stern.

Well, anyway, the magical transporter had been stowed away in the cottage, carefully hidden along with a fair number of other magical items. Selwyn had woven powerful and potent spells into each of them to mask their true natures, then he'd locked them away in a kitchen cabinet.

"You forget all about these things now, boy," he'd said. "And never speak of them."

But of course, telling any teenage boy to forget or ignore something in particular was akin to telling him not to steal cookies from the cookie jar when his mother's back was turned.

The more any boy was told not to do a thing, especially at such a rebellious age, the more tempting it became. And so it was with the transporter, too …

So, of course, he had not forgotten that device. No, he had committed it to memory instead. Though ignorant about how to operate it, he recognized that it was his sole hope of fleeing the village with his beloved sister. He'd have to find her first, however. Hopefully, the small girl would be where he last had seen her, at the cottage, snugly dressed in her bedtime attire.

He was going to make his way right back there, without further ado! And so, he tiptoed, peering around corners, sticking to the walls and the dark shadows, hiding in doorways.

As he drew closer to his abode, he abruptly halted and fixed his gaze in horror.

No! Please, no! A whimper of distress fled his throat. Yes, he saw the cottage, but the thatched roof was billowing with smoke, and the tiny windows at the front had been shattered.

He silently beseeched the gods above, hoping, praying.

"Please, God, let my sister Olesia still be alive and unhurt. Please. She's so small, so young. You can't need to take her away. My little sister's no use to you, Lord …"

He drew in a deep breath, racing towards the battered door, which hung off its hinges.

He slipped in through the entrance, surveying the wreckage before him.

The walls were scorched, the furniture was overturned, and debris was lying everywhere. The curtains had been torn down to use for setting light to the place, and the table and chairs were upside down. The legs of the chairs were all smashed, and Selwyn's wooden cabinet sat like matchsticks. And in the centre of the room lay the lifeless form of Annis, Selwyn's beloved wife.

Although her face was obscured from view, he knew the garments she wore all too well, almost always a long red dress and a blue ribbon tied like a sash at its waist. His eyes were transfixed by the sight of her body lying in a pool of her blood. He felt sick to his stomach.

Clutching firmly to the conviction that his sister had eluded a comparably grim fate, he scoured the cottage. More shattered furniture lay upturned, and he thrust his hands into the jumbled assortment of splintered wood and fine ashes, his fingers tracing tracks of desperation.

He combed through every room. "Olesia! Are you there?" he cried out, his eyes darting from one corner to another. Tears welled in his eyes. "Olesia!" he screamed, the sound of his own voice echoing through the devastated ruins of his home.

The thought that his sister might have died was almost too much to bear, but he fought against it. As if from nowhere, a faint but unmistakable sound reached his ears from beneath the stairs. A faint sound like the mewling of a newborn kitten. Some sort of plaintive and helpless thing.

He moved cautiously towards a small door and crouched to open it.

The interior was pitch black, but he could just about make out the outline.

"Oh, my God! Olesia! It's me. Come to me. Oh, my God!"

His tears finally came, as if a floodgate had opened.

With trembling hands, he reached in to pull the fragile figure from the cramped space, relief flooding through him as her small frame settled in his arms.

There was terror in her eyes and dried tracks of tears on each of her tiny cheeks. He wrapped her in a tight embrace, whispering her name before setting her on her feet and taking her hand.

Keeping his sister's hand firmly in his, he led her into the kitchen.

As he surveyed the devastation, his eyes fell upon the second small cabinet, this one being where Selwyn had kept his secret magical artefacts.

It had toppled over, its contents scattered on the ground.

Remarkably, none of the magical items had been taken as they had all been cleverly disguised as ordinary household objects. The room seemed to fill with an air of mystery; the once-hidden treasures now lay exposed, waiting to be picked up and examined.

Among the fallen artefacts lay some seemingly inconspicuous items such as a tarnished teapot, an old-looking pocket watch, and a dusty old book. Without delay, the boy also spotted a robust hessian sack conveniently positioned on the nearby floor. He promptly began to fill it with a variety of the magical items, choosing the ones he had diligently committed to memory.

As he rummaged through the mess, his hand brushed against a wooden musical recorder lying on the ground. He recognized it at once. This was the transporter Selwyn had mentioned.

He grasped it tightly. "Olesia, grab the other end and keep hold of it," he commanded.

The boy's mind raced as he held onto it, his fingers gripping it tightly.

How does it work? he wondered, desperately trying to recall any of the instructions.

Selwyn had told him many times, but had any of it sunk

into his head? No, probably not! The thing was, if Selwyn had ordered him to forget he'd ever heard the instructions, then he would have remembered them. But as it happened, Selwyn had not said a thing. So, he'd forgotten.

He closed his eyes and tried to visualise a place, any place, far from this village.

Would that transport him there? No.

His mind drew a blank; he had never left this place before and had no idea where to go in any case. He was just saying to himself, "I'll have to put some thought into remem—"

There came a hellish crash, the unmistakable sound of splintering wood. Someone had burst in through the door, rampaging through the place, treading over everything for a second time. The figure was a man, wearing a dark mask. A raider. The children's eyes were huge, and Olesia began crying again, clinging to her brother. The man's eyes cast over the teen boy and his sister.

Olesia had let her side of the wooden recorder tumble to the floor. The boy eyed it, then looked warily back at their unexpected, unwelcome visitor.

The masked raider's eyes glinted as he reached for his wand. "What have we here?"

The male's voice dripped with ill intent.

The boy grabbed his sister's hand and dashed behind the large kitchen stove that dominated the middle of the room. The raider's footsteps followed, sending judders through the space as he went; the man was huge by comparison, solid and heavy. His steps were getting closer.

The raider lifted his wand and made a quick downward motion, a slice into the air, unleashing a bolt of lightning that narrowly missed the children. It sent the light zooming above their heads and striking the wall behind. The impact caused a shower of debris to rain down on their hair, filling the air with choking dust. But this could be useful … couldn't it?

Taking advantage of the momentary distraction, the boy quickly manoeuvred himself and his sister around the stove and out of the line of fire. The raider, his vision obscured, coughed and swore, firing off a flurry of lightning bolts that seemed to manifest from every corner.

As the chaos raged around them, the boy tried to focus his mind once more on the wooden recorder in his hand. "Olesia," he whispered as he stooped to her. "Pick up the other end of the recorder, like before." She looked up, big-eyed, not knowing what to do.

With a steady hand, he placed his sister's hand on the recorder, his grip tight on her arm.

Again, he tried to recall any of Selwyn's instructions, his mind racing with confusion.

Gradually, the dust began to clear, the raider's voice echoing.

"Come out! Come out, horrible pair! Wherever you are!" His tone oozed with glee. Was this just some sort of a vile game to him? Why did he take such pleasure in it? "I will get you …"

As the dust settled completely, the raider's gaze landed on the two huddled on the floor.

The teenage boy turned his back and shielded his sister, whispering, "Don't be afraid, Olesia," in her ear to calm her trembling form.

He braced himself.

A bright bolt of lightning struck the ground beneath them, and the room began to spin wildly.

Next, they found themselves engulfed in a tidal wave of darkness, and the boy felt an intense surge of pain surging through his body.

So, this is how it feels to die.

Chapter Two:
The City of Elders

Ten years later.

As the day gave way to night, Lily found herself perched atop the ruins of an ancient wall; this place had crumbled ages ago, and its dilapidated structure, which may once have been filled with hallways and rooms, now stood surrounded by thick, forgotten woodland just beyond the city of the Elders. All that remained were these moss-covered walls and a silent, still emptiness where memories of the place's former glories had been lost to the ravages of time.

Lily's imagination ran wild. She contemplated the mysteries of the ruins beneath her, unable to help wondering what secrets were hidden within the walls, and what stories the old stones would tell if they could speak. She imagined the people who might once have resided here, picturing all their hopes and dreams, their many triumphs and tragedies.

What kind of ancient drama might have unfolded here?

Lily's slim silhouette barely cast a shadow in the gentle light of the setting sun. Her fine, light brown hair danced in loose waves around her face with the slightest breeze, while bright, clear brown eyes hinted at an understanding far beyond her thirteen years.

Lily's eyes closed as she inhaled the crisp air, her shoulders relaxing at the soothing stillness of her surroundings. Her spine tingled with a sudden chill as the wind howled, prompting the trees towering over her to sway and rustle. As the sun's final rays slowly faded, Lily hugged herself, shrouded in the familiar pang of loneliness once again.

She was all too aware that she was the last of her kind, a lone survivor.

Fortunately, Lord and Lady Walsingham had taken her in and become her loving guardians. Lord Walsingham was a respected statesman and privy councillor of the Elders, while his wife Ursula was known far and wide for her kindness. They had raised Lily as their own, showering her with care and affection, despite being unable to conceive a child of their own.

While Lily appreciated the kindness of Lord and Lady Walsingham, however, she couldn't shake off the strange and constant feeling of incompleteness.

Growing up without knowing her true lineage or cultural roots left her feeling disconnected from the world around, like a spell book with only missing pages.

Memories of her parents remained elusive, hovering on the periphery of her consciousness.

Lord and Lady Walsingham, too, were ignorant of Lily's history, save for the fact that she hailed from a clan ruthlessly annihilated by malevolent sorcerers. The thought of such a terrible crime was hideous, and she often wondered sadly about her parents' fate.

Although mostly content with the Walsinghams, Lily had a persistent feeling that they were hiding something; a haunting shadow seemed to be always by her side. But on the other hand, what was to say that it was not just the imagination of a disenfranchised girl?

With a background like Lily's, perhaps it was not surprising she would be prone to dreams.

Lily was now part of the Elders, an ancient clan of people who had given up the use of magic, although she found their history fascinating. More than two centuries ago, they had endured a devastating civil war that had nearly eradicated their entire community.

This cataclysm had led them to a certain understanding, which was that unchecked magic—like a huge wild horse turned loose in a crowded marketplace—was a peril indeed, particularly in the hands of the wrong individuals. In response, they had instituted a series of laws gradually restricting and eventually prohibiting the practice of magic within the realm.

Only a small group of members, all men possessing an innate magical ability, were ever permitted to wield it, but solely under strict parameters set by the law. A feeling of irritation surged within Lily; why was only a minuscule assembly of 'privileged men' allowed to wield magic? That was despicable! These select few underwent rigorous training and education to serve as guardians of the realm, tasked with safeguarding their people in case of external threats or potential invasions. But hadn't the Elders' city itself already stood for centuries, fortified by the ancient magic of incredible potency, rendering it impervious to external forces?

No one had restricted magic in the olden days, had they? It was preposterous!

So, Lily despised the strict laws and silly notions preventing her from practising magic too.

The consequences of breaking these laws, though, were severe, ranging from hefty fines to public floggings, imprisonment, or even death in cases where harmful spells or curses were cast.

Some punishments seemed especially ridiculous.

Take the case of Ms Wigglebout, for example; she was a middle-aged spinster who had committed minor offences on purpose, specifically with the aim of receiving five public lashings from Mr Suckerworth! He was a flogger, one for whom she had developed an infatuation.

Her repeated infractions had eventually angered the local authorities.

They had threatened to lock her up and throw away the key, leaving poor Mr Suckerworth to carry out his many public floggings in peace.

Lily did not crave such floggings, nor any other form of stupid punishment. No, Lily lived in constant anxiety of being caught by someone else—the anti-magic authorities.

Despite the risks, she was determined to learn. Simple charms, curses, divination, potions, and other seemingly innocuous forms of magic had become her refuge lately.

Lily would spend most of her time outside the city, in the ruins, a place where she could freely practise the magic she had gleaned from books in the city library, meant only for academic purposes. Alternatively, she would borrow books from Lord Walsingham's personal collection.

Wasn't there something wonderfully special about the power of love potions?

She brewed them using ingredients foraged and scavenged from the forest.

Lily enjoyed causing mischief and mayhem, such as making her school enemies fall in love with each other or temporarily afflicting the pretty or mean girls with hideous warts on their noses. People were suspicious, of course. Magic had to be involved in this unless there was some peculiar nose-wart virus going around. It seemed unlikely. Anyway, no one suspected Lily.

Unfortunately, despite Lily's passion for magic being unwavering, her level of expertise was rudimentary at best.

It would take her hours to execute even a simple spell, often working late into the night.

Without proper instruction, Lily feared, she would never truly advance. For now, she was alone with her ruminations and her dreams, and she would have to make the best of things.

Here among the ruins, Lily also found comfort from the escalating tension within the city walls. Strict curfews had recently been imposed, the protectors more frequently patrolling the streets, watching everyone with intense scrutiny. It made her feel even more uneasy.

These snooping patrols were making it harder for her to leave the city, for sure.

Day after day, there seemed to be more and more frustrating limitations.

Lily's thoughts—again—were drifting to her first love, her magic.

It freed her from the mundane and strict world within the Elders' realm, and the prospect of mastering it gave her comfort. If she could only master it for herself, then she would have created a connection to her parents and people. Lily would be back where she belonged.

But it was even more than that, the language of magic transcending culture and heritage.

It was a means to connect with something greater than herself, to tap into the power of the universe, and thus have a chance to create something beautiful and pure.

***

As Lord Walsingham strode towards Lily's chambers at Walsingham Manor in the ancient city of the Elders, his tall and lean form commanded attention.

His sharp facial features showed a serious expression, and his short, wavy hair now bore grey wisps that added to his distinguished appearance.

Dressed in all black, he exuded a commanding presence that brooked no argument.

The hallway leading to Lily's room was adorned with intricate tapestries depicting the Elders' history and artistry, but Lord Walsingham barely even gave these a side glance as he passed.

Staring straight ahead, his thoughts seemed perpetually consumed by worries about Lily's safety. The girl was growing up far too fast, and with her advancing years also came an advancing inquisitiveness, the sort of thing prone to getting girls like Lily into trouble.

Pushing open the heavy wooden door to her chamber, Lord Walsingham met with silence.

"Oh! For goodness' sake! Please, not again!" he cried out, exasperated.

Though accustomed to Lily's sneaking out, the quiet was still unsettling and irritating. Yes, he knew this room inside and out, and he recognised every sound—or lack of it— within it.

The only sound tonight was the gentle rustling of curtains stirred by a cool and increasing breeze that wafted in through the open window. The room was dimly lit by flickering candles scattered throughout, casting shadows that danced on the walls.

Nowhere, nowhere at all, was Lily.

Lord Walsingham's keen eyes surveyed the room, taking in every detail. His attention fell upon a cluttered wooden desk near the slightly open window, where sheets of paper, ink bottles, and quills lay in disarray. Amidst the chaos, he noticed a pencil drawing that Lily herself had created, a stunning depiction of a small village with a towering building sitting atop a hill.

Tearing his gaze away from the drawing, Lord Walsingham retraced his steps towards the door, and without delay, he returned to his study.

For now, he would have to forget all about young Lily sneaking out in the evenings like this.

He had far more serious and pressing matters demanding his immediate attention.

These were perilous times. Political turmoil was rampant, bubbling like a cauldron and affecting every aspect of daily life. Anxiety and uncertainty had taken hold of the Elders' realms, also of the other realms still standing against Abaddon and his army.

The Elders' realm, believed to be the primary target of Abaddon, had lately been rife with rumours, whispers, and with the speculation of secret alliances, hidden feuds, and potential treaties, only adding to the already tense atmosphere hanging in the air like a suffocating fog.

Despite the ancient enchantment protecting the realm, it was clear that Abaddon would eventually find a way to circumvent it. Abaddon wouldn't hesitate to strike and Lord Walsingham's realm was, as yet anyway, ill-prepared for the soon ensuing onslaught.

The fate of the realm was hanging in the balance, and Walsingham couldn't afford to be caught off guard. And what's more, he had no intention of allowing it either.

He would take all necessary precautions to ensure that Abaddon didn't find what he was looking for. The next few hours would be fraught with danger, but he remained resolute.

Lord Walsingham settled into his chair in the study, his gaze fixed firmly on the door.

Shortly, his guest should be arriving.

***

Lily leapt off the wall onto the uneven ground, scanning the area for a small rock. After a few minutes of sifting through the dirt, she found a pebble that suited her and placed it on top of one of the ruins, which looked like the remains of a pillar from a once great hall.

She focused her mind on the rock and chanted a spell.

Over and over, she said the same, focusing, hoping, pleading with the universe.

The wind blew, rustling through the leaves of the wood like waves on a shore, but still the minuscule rock remained in place when Lily tried to move it with only magic's force.

Out of nowhere, a movement in the woods broke her concentration, her head snapping up, her eyes sharply focusing on what had caught her eye.

It was the figure of a boy, someone she was sure she recognized, even in the dark.

"Robert, how many times do I have to tell you to stay away when I'm practising magic?"

Lily's frustrated voice cleaved through the ruins.

Sure enough, there was Robert, her neighbour and partner in crime, with his unruly brown hair and mischievous grin. He now stood right in front of her, emerging from the trees like some sort of wood nymph. He wore his habitual cheeky dimpled smile.

He had a penchant for shadowing her everywhere, and they relished clambering together along the city roofs or raiding the nearby market stalls for apples and pears.

"But didn't I tell you—three times, actually—not to be near me when I'm practising magic?"

Robert just looked up with his piercing eyes, innocently pushing all the boundaries she'd set.

"Robert," she tried again. "If you keep hanging around me, then I'm afraid you'll end up in serious trouble. Or maybe both of us will."

"Okay," he said for about the twentieth time of being chastised for the very same thing.

But in secret, Lily harboured a worry—a worry that she might accidentally cause him harm. Once, she had tried to cast a harmless spell to change the colour of a frog, but it had backfired spectacularly, rebounding on a hiding Robert lurking behind one of the stone ruins.

His hair stayed a bright shade of orange for a whole week, leaving his parents flabbergasted and dumbfounded, unable to explain the strange occurrence.

"I'm sure it's something in the water, Mother," he had said, looking all innocent as always, something he was really good at. "I think you'll have to complain about it."

Now, Robert peeked out from behind some bushes, his eyes widening with excitement as he sprang up, his thin frame moving quickly towards her.

Lily shot him a stern glance. "You know very well that if they catch us out here practising magic together, we'll be in serious trouble," she chided.

Robert hung his head as if in great in remorse. "Okay. Sorry, Lily."

Okay, okay, okay. If he said 'okay' again, she would explode! "Please, stop saying okay when I tell you not to do something. Stop saying okay, and please *start* following what I say."

Her cheeks were mottled with annoyance.

"Okay," he said, and chuckled.

She moved toward him, making a swatting motion as if to slap him playfully. "Oh, stop!"

She softened her expression, offering a resigned smile as she took his hand.

"Come on. Let's go. It's getting late."

As Lily and Robert made their way back to the city, they strolled through the dense woodland and up the hill, where the breathtaking panorama of the Elders' city greeted them once again.

The grandeur of the cityscape from this hilltop always left Lily spellbound. It was a beautiful vantage point ever everything they knew, a view of the vivid sky as it kissed the landscape.

The diverse buildings, each with its own unique shape and size, melded seamlessly with one another, presenting a remarkable sight. The intricate web of streets and alleyways meandered like a serene stream, weaving together into a mesmerising tapestry kissing the horizon.

Despite the brewing tensions simmering within the Elders' Kingdom, the flickering lanterns adorning all the pathways cast a warm and inviting radiance, enveloping the entire city in a resplendent aura impossible to ignore, even with the lurking tensions concealed in shadow.

Lily and Robert hurried through the narrow streets and alleys, and into the softly lit town square, where the rotund town crier's voice resonated like a solemn bell.

He stood high and resplendent on a wooden platform, bathed in the glow of two sizeable gas lanterns suspended from tall wooden poles positioned on each side of the stage. His ruddy cheeks added a distinctively jovial look to his face as he called out the latest happenings from on high.

Dressed in a jet-black gown and a flowing crimson cloak, he also bore a tall rectangular top hat and sturdy wooden staff, each item adding weight to his authoritative appearance.

"Dear citizens of the Elders' Kingdom. Some among us aim to cause chaos and distrust. But I assure you, we will not let them succeed!" A great cry went up from the cheering crowd.

As the crier's voice thundered on, it stirred a collective sense of unity and resolve. Many responded with approving nods, others in the assembly enthusiastically shouting, "Yes!"

Buoyed by the response, the crier continued, his voice growing more alive and resonant.

"As for the rumours of poisonings, our law enforcers are tirelessly working to apprehend the culprits behind these heinous crimes. They shall not rest until justice is served, and our people once again find safety. While fear and uncertainty may plague other realms, we, the people of the Elders' Kingdom, shall not yield to such emotions. Guided by our wise High Councillor, Lothar, who leads with unparalleled wisdom and courage, we stand firm, unwavering, and resolute!"

Amidst the lively throng, Lily and Robert navigated slowly through the crowd, the crier's words providing a backdrop. Out of excitement, someone in the crowd enthusiastically exclaimed, "Yes!" and unintentionally nudged Lily's head, eliciting an annoyed "Ouch."

Slowly, they made their way through the crowds to Walsingham Manor, Lily and Robert deftly manoeuvring through dimly lit and empty streets, skilfully evading the watchful sentries periodically seen patrolling the cobblestone pathways. It was a delightful game for them, a secret challenge to test their stealth and cunning. They found immense amusement in these sneaky exploits, sharing mischievous grins as they relished the excitement of slipping past each guard.

Lily and Robert loitered outside Walsingham Manor.

"Well, I suppose I ought to make my way home," Robert admitted, his expression downcast. "Anyway, I bet you're sick of me hanging about. That's what you always say."

They laughed.

Lily, her arms folded, proposed an alternative with a shrug and a grin. "Or you could partner with me in purloining a slice of cream cake from the pantry? I'll tolerate you five minutes more."

Robert's face illuminated with mischief, his decision evident. Together, they crafted a clever strategy to infiltrate the kitchen pantry and secure an illicit share of cream cake.

As they tiptoed through the dimly lit hallway, the enticing scent of freshly baked pastries wafted towards them, tantalising their senses and stirring their hunger.

Their sharp eyes scanned the hallway, seeking out the

door to the pantry.

Intent on their mission, the thought of indulging in a creamy slice of cake made their mouths water with anticipation. They were about to turn the corner into the kitchen, but Lily's eyes squinted. "Ssh," she whispered. Robert stopped dead in his tracks. Lily looked so serious.

Lily had caught sight of something peculiar; the door to Lord Walsingham's study was slightly ajar, a flicker of light seeping through the small gap.

It was strange that Lord Walsingham was still in his study at this hour, as he usually preferred to conduct his affairs upstairs in his bedroom chamber, pretending to listen to Ursula gossiping about her daily social gatherings. Lily's curiosity was piqued.

She couldn't resist the temptation to investigate further. "Secret meeting?" she whispered to Robert and they quickly hid behind a thick wooden door.

They peeked through a small gap in an attempt to see what was happening inside the study.

It was filled with warm, flickering light from the roaring fire. A jolly and plump man with a head of silver-white hair stood before it, his cheeks aglow with rosy colour.

In an instant, Lily recognized him.

"Lord Cecil!" she whispered to Robert who edged close so he could hear. "That's Lord Walsingham's friend." Indeed, the man was Walsingham's dearest and most trusted friend. Lily had always liked him too, as one of the few adults who'd taken a genuine interest in her drawing.

Lord Cecil gazed intently at a portrait hanging above the fireplace, an image of a stern-looking man in sombre black attire, with a neatly trimmed moustache and a waistcoat with a stunning timepiece on a chain. This was a painting of Lord Walsingham's late father, a distinguished figure. The neat white collar drew attention to the man's deep, piercing brown eyes.

As Lord Cecil stood before the imposing portrait of Senior Lord Walsingham, he appeared to be performing a comical dance. He shifted his weight from left to right, his feet shuffling nervously as if trying to dodge the intense gaze of the painted figure.

Lily and Robert exchanged a subtle grin, and this seemed to spur Lily into pressing her ear against the solid oak door. "No, no. It has to be tonight," her guardian said.

Though muffled, the urgency in his voice was clear. Lily could feel a knot forming in her stomach; whatever he was discussing, it seemed to be a matter of great importance.

"Tonight?" Lord Cecil questioned, turning his gaze away from the painting.

Lily could now see Lord Walsingham stepping into view towards the glinting fireplace.

"Yes, I'm afraid it's a matter of great urgency," Lord Walsingham replied, heaving a sigh. "You must have heard the rumours in the streets, those vile and heinous words. They say there are young girls being poisoned, some reported missing. It's only a matter of time, my friend."

Lord Cecil seemed troubled by the news and sank into one of the two brown leather armchairs angled towards the fireplace. However, his attention was quickly diverted to the pastry nibbles on a silver tray, resting on a small table between the two chairs. He helped himself to one of the nibbles, holding it up to his face to examine it before swallowing it whole.

As Lord Walsingham turned toward the crackling fire, the dancing flames illuminated his demeanour with flickering shadows. He reached for the fire poker and, with a deft movement, prodded at the glowing embers, causing an array of sparks to fly up and dance in the air.

They made quite a show, just like a thousand fireflies.

"We both know Abaddon will do anything to kill off the Norn's prophecy," he said, his voice low and ominous, the words laden with meaning.

Lord Cecil replied in a mumbled tone, his words too indistinct for Lily and Robert to catch.

She watched as Lord Walsingham considered his colleague's response, his brow furrowing in thought. Finally, he replaced the fire poker in its holder, sinking down into the plush seat opposite Lord Cecil's. As he settled in, Lily could see that he looked troubled.

The lines on his face showed much worry.

"That bloody tyrant Abaddon and his goblins have plunged five of the nine realms into war," Lord Walsingham affirmed, his voice low and intense.

Lily strained to hear the rest of what he was saying.

Robert leaned in closer to Lily, his curiosity piqued. "What are they talking about?" he whispered, his eyes fixed on the door. "I can't make it out."

Lily shook her head slowly, her gaze still fixed on Lord Cecil and Lord Walsingham. "I don't know exactly. But it sounds important," she whispered back. "Hush, let me listen."

As Lord Walsingham spoke again, his voice was fretful, only adding to the gravity of his words. "Our High Councillor Lothar's once virtuous mind has been twisted and corrupted by Abaddon. The Kingdom sits on the brink of collapse, and I fear for Lily's safety once it does."

Lily recoiled, her eyes large and full of shock.

Lord Walsingham's words had an urgency that was palpable, his concern for Lily's safety evident in every syllable. "As soon as Lily returns, you must leave tonight. We cannot take any chances," he said, his gaze unwavering as he looked at Lord Cecil.

As Lord Cecil leaned in closer to Lord Walsingham, his voice dropped to a hushed tone now barely audible to Robert and Lily by the doorway. "Does he know you plan to move her?"

Lord Walsingham hesitated before answering. "Not yet. Actually, I've been unable to locate him. But I've sent word." After this, he paused, deep in thought. "I know I'm asking a great deal of you, but I trust no one else for this task," he urged. "I hope you understand."

Lord Cecil reclined in his seat, his expression as calm as ever. "Very well. Then tonight it is. I'll do everything in my power to protect her. You can depend on me to do so."

"Good. It's settled then," Lord Walsingham said, so much relief in his voice.

Lily watched on as she saw Lord Walsingham stand and approach the fireplace. He took an iron fire poker and moved from near Lily's vantage point.

Lily and Robert now both had their ears pressed against the door, trying to catch any sound, but hearing only silence. The door flew open, causing the two children who had been pressed against it to fall to the floor.

They looked up to see Lord Walsingham, holding a fire poker above his head in surprise. "Lily! Robert!" he exclaimed, lowering the iron. "What the devil are you up to?"

"Sir," Lily replied, embarrassed that she had been caught.

***

Lily sat in the armchair opposite Lord Cecil who smiled at her warmly. Lord Walsingham was leading young Robert out of the room, his arms around the boy's shoulder.

"Robert, not a word of what you heard tonight to anyone, you hear me?"

The boy stared up, nodding silently.

"Not even your parents. If you tell anyone, I need you to know that you could endanger Lily's life. Do you understand?" he warned sternly, and the boy again vigorously nodded.

"Yes, sir. I won't say a word." Robert's voice was feeble. Listening at the doorway had been fun, but now, the look on his pallid face showed that he may have been regretting it.

"Good. We will talk tomorrow. Now hurry home before your parents start to worry," the man added briskly. Robert looked up at Lord Walsingham a second time, catching the man's gaze.

"They have probably not noticed I've been gone, sir," he said and smiled, glancing over at Lily before muttering a dejected, "Goodbye," as he left. After his departure, Lord Walsingham made his way back to Lord Cecil and Lily, stopping before the fireplace, his back turned to her.

"I know all this must be hard to understand but …" he began.

"Why are they killing young girls? And in any case, what does any of that have to do with me?" Lily interrupted before he could even finish.

Lord Walsingham sighed, contemplating a well-suited reply.

"Because, you see, people … adults … Sometimes, they can be incredibly cruel. And …" Lord Walsingham paused, taking a moment to choose his words carefully. "Abaddon and his followers are targeting young girls they believe a Norm's prophecy might pertain to. Abaddon is firmly convinced that this prophecy is somehow tied to his own destiny."

His voice was filled with profound sadness. He approached her and knelt beside her seat, placing a gentle hand on her shoulder as if bidding farewell. But their moment was interrupted as the door to the study creaked open and then shut again, shattering the stillness of the room.

Ursula entered the study, her eyes fixed on Lily as she approached, a smile gracing her lips despite the pain she was trying so hard to conceal.

Lord Walsingham moved aside, allowing Ursula to kneel before Lily, offering her a small rucksack and pulling her into a tight embrace.

Ursula hugged her tightly, a single tear cascading down her cheek; she tried to wipe it off before Lily could notice.

Lily had never witnessed Ursula shedding tears, although she did remember that on one occasion, she had seen Ursula bravely stepping in when an enraged villager had targeted the privy council, with Lord Walsingham as the intended victim.

Ursula had shielded her husband from harm, and the scar on her right forearm bore witness to her bravery. Despite the pain, Ursula had not shed a tear, making the single, undeniable tear now rolling down her cheek all the more striking to Lily.

"I want to stay and fight," Lily declared, her

determination shining through her words. "I won't leave you," she added with growing confidence. "I will help to protect you."

Lord Walsingham gave a sly smile, his pride in her courage evident.

"Lily, it's not us he wants though, so you must think about yourself first and foremost. It's you he desires. We'll be fine, and your safety is of paramount importance. So, it's wiser for you to accompany Lord Cecil. He's well-travelled and well-connected," he asserted, his tone resolute. "You'll become virtually untraceable, leaving no trail for Abaddon to follow."

"But what about you two? Who will protect you?" Lily asked. "Abaddon will come looking, won't he?"

Lord Walsingham gave a tight smile. "We'll be all right, Lily; once Abaddon realises you aren't here, he will not … At least, I hope …" He was floundering for an answer to give her, one that would not be a lie. "Well, look, you don't have to worry about—"

"I heard what you said! I'm not a little girl anymore. I want to protect you," Lily said with fiery determination.

"Listen to us, Lily. We're doing this because we love you, and we want to keep you safe," Ursula said, placing a hand on Lily's shoulder. "The more you argue against it, the harder you are making it. You can help us best by doing as Lord Walsingham says."

Lily thrashed away as if stung. "No! I won't leave. There's nothing you or anyone can do about it."

"Please, Lily," Ursula pleaded, her voice trembling.

Lily exhaled heavily, exaggerating the sound.

"Well, if I go, when will it be safe for me to come back?" she asked with a touch of anxiety.

"When it's safe," Lord Walsingham responded. There was sadness in his tone.

"You are a brave girl," Ursula stuttered sadly, tears flowing freely.

Lily, knowing that she had no choice, nodded with reluctance.

Ursula smiled weakly, saying, "Promise me you'll listen to Lord Cecil and do everything he asks. Please don't ask too many questions because these take time, and … Just listen to him, that's all, Lily. Please. Sometimes, stubbornly arguing can lose time and put you at risk."

Her face showed the unspoken, *and you may not always have time.*

Lily, knowing that she had no choice, nodded reluctantly.

"She has to go," Lord Walsingham said softly, squeezing his wife's shoulder. Ursula held Lily in her arms as if not wanting to let go.

"Ursula. It's time for the girl to make a move," he continued, reaching for Lily's hand and giving it a rather tight squeeze.

He looked into her large brown eyes, Lily believing she could see hope in his expression.

She stood there, feeling the weight of the moment, understanding both the urgency and the rationale behind their decisions, even if it meant leaving behind everything she knew.

"Lord Cecil will keep you safe. Together, you will move around using port keys, secret magical objects that can transport you to different locations! It'll be like an adventure for you, Lily. However, to ensure your safety, you must leave with Lord Cecil tonight."

Chapter Three:
The Port Key

With a sudden creaking sound, the rear entrance door swung open, and Lily and Lord Cecil emerged into the chilly night air. They crossed the grounds of Walsingham's manor, with Robert following them discreetly like a pup unwilling to be parted from his new owner.

Despite the darkness, Robert strained his eyes to keep them in sight as they approached a disused and decrepit stone staircase at the rear of the property. Careful not to make a sound, he ducked in behind one of the weathered pillars to avoid being seen. He was determined not to let Lily get away so easily, and he was good at stealth, so … Robert would try, anyway.

The staircase led up to a small and insignificant balcony, partially obscured by overgrown weeds and tangled undergrowth. Vines snaked their way up the balcony's sides, and gangly unkempt weeds sprouted defiantly from every nook and cranny in the stonework.

Robert's curiosity was piqued. What could be driving Lily and Lord Cecil to ascend the stairs to such an unremarkable location? Despite his curiosity, Robert stayed quiet, trailing after them as they climbed. The balcony was devoid of any notable features, save for the small marble stone in its centre. Lily and Lord Cecil moved towards it with purpose, and Robert stood holding his breath and watched from the shadows, waiting to see what would happen next.

"Are you ready, Lily?" Lord Cecil asked, and she gave a hesitant nod, exhaling sharply. "Touch the stone," he said and gestured as he placed his hand on the stone, and she did the same.

As her palm touched the cold, smooth surface, a glimmering green light instantly enveloped them; it was as bright as an emerald sun, darting as if piercing into her skull, and she pulled her hand away to shield her eyes. The moment her hand left the stone, everything went pitch black.

Lily felt around herself, her sensitive eyes clearly taking a moment to adjust.

Then, she gazed around the darkness until her eyes levelled on Lord Cecil, who seemed to be fixated on something else. She stared hard, as if attempting to make out what he was staring at.

Robert noticed she visibly recoiled. Yes, she had seen the very small figure standing a few feet away. She was staring at Robert himself!

***

"Robert! You total idiot! What on earth have you done?" Lord Cecil yelled, closing in on him while he trembled and wondered whether he should run or stay put. "You stupid, dumb boy!"

Robert just kicked at the ground, scattering the tiny stones underfoot, scuffing his shoes.

"You're not supposed to be here! Do you realise the danger you have put yourself in, along with Lily?" Lord Cecil bellowed with annoyance. "And your parents? Do you think your absence wouldn't raise an alarm? Once they figure out that you're missing, they will realise that Lily has disappeared as well. How could you do this? It's only a matter of time now before Abaddon connects you to her and comes after us! You are a silly, silly boy!"

His frustrated bellowing was making Robert's body quake with terror, tears silently tracing their path down his cheeks.

"Lily's my friend," said Robert in a small voice. "If she's in danger, I want to help her."

He knew if Lily had been in his place, she would have done the same for him.

Lord Cecil heaved a defeated sigh.

"Robert, it's a noble thought but far too dangerous. I wish you would have stayed back, but there's nothing we can do about it now; the port key can't be used in reverse. We must keep moving. The two of you must always stay by my side, no tricks. And you, Robert, you must do as I say at all times, no moaning about it. Do you understand?"

He raised a brow, and Robert gave a firm nod.

Lord Cecil looked around now, finally taking in the grassy empty field in which they now found themselves. "We should be safe for now," he said briskly. "Come along, there's an inn in the town not far from here." He began leading the two children from the empty field and all the way into the town until they arrived at the inn.

The inn's exterior was bathed in the soft, golden glow of antique lanterns, exuding a warm and inviting ambiance. The inn itself was a quaint two-story building, made of stone that seemed to absorb the moonlight, giving it a silvery-blue hue.

A wooden sign bearing the name 'The Moonlit Tavern' swung gently in the breeze above the door, its painted letters catching the lantern light and casting elegant shadows.

Lily stared as if she found it charming, so different from the stone buildings she was used to.

Lord Cecil ushered the children into the inn, offering a gentle bow to the lady innkeeper.

She was a plump middle-aged woman with a face like a sour lemon; she looked up from her ledger with a sharp glare, as if the trio had interrupted something incredibly important.

"We require board for the night," Lord Cecil said, producing a handful of gold coins from his pocket and placing them on the counter with a metallic jingle.

The innkeeper stared approvingly at the coin collection, then looked up at Lord Cecil.

Her expression softened into a smile, revealing gaps in her front teeth.

"As it 'appens, oi 'as a room with two beds on the second floor. The bath 'ouse is on the same floor, an' there's a lav at the end of the 'all. Breakfast will be served from sunrise till mid-mornin', Mr ..." she said, handing Lord Cecil a brass key, brushing her hand against his flirtatiously.

Lord Cecil was momentarily flustered by her touch but managed to compose himself.

"It's Mr ... Key, Mr Lowkey," he lied, fabricating things as he went along, ill prepared.

The innkeeper's eyes twinkled mischievously. "Well, Mr Lowkey, if there's anyfink else you needs, you just gives me an 'oller, a'right?" she said with a wink and a grin.

Lord Cecil, uncertain how to respond, offered a courteous response.

"No, that will be all. Thank you." He then shifted his focus to Lily and Robert, who appeared confused. He suggested, "Shall we go get some rest? What do you say?"

Lily and Robert followed Lord Cecil up the narrow stairs, their weariness finally catching up to them. The room they entered was small yet cosy, with a quaint window overlooking the town square. Two narrow beds were pushed against opposite walls, with a wooden chest at the foot of each bed, and a small rug covering the creaky floorboards.

"Make yourselves at home," Lord Cecil said, gesturing to the beds. "I will go down to the common room and see about finding us some supper."

As he left the room, Lily and Robert exchanged a worried glance.

The night's events had left them exhausted and on edge. Robert sank down onto one of the beds, his head in his hands, and let out a heavy sigh. "This bed is mine," he announced as if waiting for Lily to giggle as she usually would. But this time, she did not.

He was feeling as if he had done the most stupid, ridiculous thing by trying to stalk Lily to wherever it was she was headed to. "I can't believe I've put you and my parents in danger like this," he said, his voice barely above a whisper. "He's right. I'm a stupid boy."

"It's all right, Robert. We're in this together," Lily said, moving to sit down beside him. "Anyway, I would have done the same in your position. It must have been a terrible shock for you, all happening so fast and with me disappearing like that. I'm actually glad you came."

Robert's chest puffed out. Lily wasn't mad at him. It was a massive relief.

But this was not the boy's sole worry. There was plenty more to panic about.

"But what if Abaddon finds us? What if we never make it back home?" Robert's voice trembled, and his eyes glistened with unshed tears.

Lily's did too.

By her face, Robert could see that Lily felt her own anxiety rising.

She probably doesn't want to add to my own worries, he thought, but said nothing about it. *I feel so silly, such an idiot.*

Lily took a noisy deep breath and placed a reassuring hand on his shoulder. "We'll do everything we can to stay safe and make it back home," he heard her say. "Robert, please stop worrying. It's done now; you're here, and I for one am glad of your company! We have each other, and Lord Cecil has a plan in place. We can get through this together. Can't we?"

Her big eyes stared down into his.

Robert nodded, clearly taking comfort from Lily's words. "I—thank you. I'm still sorry though, for what I did. But I won't talk about it again." He sniffled.

They sat in silence for a few moments, each lost in their own thoughts, hand in hand.

"Lily," he said after a while.

"What?" She looked down at the top of his head.

"I need my hand back to wipe the snot away."

Lily chuckled, releasing his hand which must have been quite numb by now; she'd been holding onto it so hard, deeply glad to have her friend at her side.

She rummaged in her pocket. "Here. Have this."

She passed him a white, folded cloth handkerchief. "It's clean. No need to give it back."

They both chuckled.

The room was quiet except for the faint sound of the howling gale outside. Despite Robert's welcome presence and his company, Lily couldn't shake the feeling of dread that had settled deep in the pit of her stomach, roiling like a knot of vipers.

***

As Lily drifted into the abyss of her recurring nightmare, twisted and distorted images flitted through her mind with a haunting liveliness.

They seemed be mocking her in her attempts to comprehend them.

Yet, amid this chaos of shifting shapes and flickering shades, an all-too-familiar and vivid scene emerged from the depths of her subconscious.

The face of an older boy appeared before her, showing urgency and desperation as he darted his eyes around, scanning the darkness as if searching for an exit from this sinister realm.

As if in response to his silent plea, lightning bolts illuminated the void above, casting eerie shadows that seemed to dance and writhe on the ground below. The air was thick with electricity, making Lily cold with fear, also making the fine hairs on her arms stand on end.

With a jarring sense of disorientation, Lily felt her reality shift and twist, as though the very fabric of the universe were shifting and warping around her.

She stumbled and tripped as she was violently thrust into an unfamiliar world, her surroundings morphing into an endless expanse of tall river reeds, swaying ominously in the howling wind. The rustling of the reeds was like a whispering choir, urging her to flee.

But she couldn't flee, could she, not when the boy was

there with her.

Even in sleep, her mind sought respite, only to keep seeing the peculiarly distorted image of that older boy again. There was no way to escape him, from how he was taking over her mind.

Blood seeped from his clothes, trickling down his white hand and fingertips, staining the soft earth beneath them; she saw no wounds, yet his severely injured body radiated tangible fear.

As she watched, the scarlet droplets started to drip slowly down from the boy, as if time itself had slowed to allow her to witness and absorb this most macabre spectacle. Each drop descended in a deliberate manner, tracing a crimson arc through the air before splattering onto the soft earth below. The sound of the drops hitting the ground was like an ancient clock, ticking away the remaining moments of their time in this twisted, unfamiliar world.

The rustling of leaves and creaking of branches pulsed as if the very world itself were alive and conspiring against them. Then, from out of nowhere, an image of a towering creature with wolf-like features appeared before them. Its eyes glowed like embers, and its sleek black fur glistened in the eerie light. Lily was seized with terror, but the creature did not lunge or bare its teeth. Instead, it merely stood there, watching with an unnerving detachment, as if waiting for some unseen signal. And then, just as quickly as the creature had appeared, it dissipated, leaving the bewildered Lily completely alone once more.

Darkness crept in from all around, swallowing everything in its path.

Lily tried to call out, to scream for help, but her voice

caught in her throat which was parched.

The darkness was suffocating, coddling her like a shroud. She felt as though she was falling, tumbling endlessly into a void, the same way everything relentlessly spins after a head injury.

***

But soon, fine beads of sweat glistened on her forehead as she jolted awake with a gasp, her eyes brimming with tears. Blinking rapidly, she wiped away the moisture that had pooled on her cheeks with trembling hands. She hesitated for a moment, listening for any signs of movement in the room. All was still. It felt as if she was entirely alone. *I hope not*, she thought.

Taking a deep breath, Lily attempted to settle back into bed, but her mind was too unsettled to allow her to rest. The room was still and quiet, but she knew she couldn't go back to sleep now.

As she got up, the floorboards creaked beneath her feet, creating a sensation of creepiness, even more than before. She glanced around; the room was indeed empty just as she'd thought, and her eyes fell on the small rucksack Ursula had prepared for her.

I will have a look at whatever's inside my bag, she thought, seeking solace and comfort.

She was hoping the bag would remind her of where she had come from and would hopefully help to stop her heart pounding as if she were running from a whole pack of tigers.

She slowly unzipped the biggest pocket of the rucksack; it held only her clothes.

They had all been folded with care. She fumbled through them, searching for something to change into, and unearthed a green knitted cardigan, a creation of Ursula's own skilled hands.

It wrapped Lily in a cocoon of comfort and safety; even the sweet smell of the washing soap was reassuring. It smelled like home, like a place filled with warmth, safety and security.

Lily cautiously made her way downstairs, her footsteps light on the wooden steps.

Towards the bottom, she was sure she heard Lord Cecil's booming laughter, and she quickened her pace, eager to join both him and her friend, Robert.

When she reached the dining room, she found Lord Cecil and Robert sitting around a substantial oak table, their plates heaped with an assortment of mouthwatering dishes.

They both looked up.

"Lily!" Robert cried as if he hadn't seen her for weeks. He ran up to her and gave a hug. "We thought you'd sleep all day," Robert quipped. "I was going to eat all your breakfast."

"Good morning, Lily," said Lord Cecil, less exuberant but still with fondness. He was speaking in a muffled voice, his mouth still stuffed with food.

"We're sorry for not waking you. You appeared to need extra sleep. Yes, quite dead to the world, you appeared."

After that nightmarish dream, Lily didn't want to think about sleep or hear about death. She was quite creeped out. A good breakfast was just what she needed, or at least a nice hot drink.

Lily eased herself into the seat across from Robert, offering him a big smile.

He grinned back.

The morning light peeked through the shades of the window at the back of the dining room, creating shapes on the large oak table situated in the centre of the room. The table was a feast for the eyes, laden with an array of tantalising fruits, crusty bread, succulent meats of all kinds, and a variety of beverages such as tea, milk, coffee, and juices, all served in huge jugs.

The aroma of freshly cooked food filled the room, creating a homely atmosphere.

"Help yourself, help yourself!" Lord Cecil said cheerfully. "In fact, if you hadn't got out of bed soon, young Lily, I'm agree we would have eaten it all. You foiled our plan in good time!"

Lord Cecil probably could have eaten most of that food, too, if they'd let him.

Lily and Robert shared a look and broke into giggles at Lord Cecil's impressive appetite.

His plate was piled four times as high as Robert's, yet he had already eaten one breakfast.

Lily fixed Lord Cecil with a resolute gaze, obviously waiting for him to discuss the day. Her gaze bore into him as if trying to mind read, wanting to know what they would do next.

He paused mid-bite, his demeanour taking on a weighty seriousness.

Clearly, he understood how to interpret her serious stare into his very soul.

"This is neither the time nor place to talk about … Well, you know," he murmured, leaning in closer, his words barely audible beyond the table. "We have to be careful about what we say to each other, even here. We cannot trust anyone. But when the time is right, we will talk."

He paused, grabbing Lily's hand and squeezing it tightly. "For now, we just eat, all right?"

She nodded.

"You brave, brave girl," Lord Cecil said to Lily, in a manner reminiscent of the words of Ursula before she had left Lord Walsingham's.

His voice seemed to be full of admiration and respect.

"Do not forget that you have people who care for you deeply, and we will do everything in our power to keep you safe." Lord Cecil leaned in closer to Lily. "However, there is one thing that is bothering me. To traverse a portal, one requires consent from its creator. Thus, he must have anticipated Robert might follow you. Do you see where I am coming from?"

Lily gave Lord Cecil a curious look, slowly nodding. Then she asked, "He?"

Lord Cecil leaned back into his wooden chair, knowing he had already said too much. "When it's safe to talk, Lily, I promise to tell you everything. Like I said, enjoy this fine breakfast."

He had already said enough for Lily, and it had put her off her food. She pushed away her plate with her hand, staring at the uneaten breakfast that only made her stomach lurch.

Puzzled glances were exchanged between Lily and Robert, and Lily's mind whirled with questions. *Who is this 'he'?* she asked herself.

Why would he create magical port keys for me to travel through?

Is he a friend of Lord Walsingham's? How did he know Robert would follow me?

Her mind was now dizzy with unanswered questions she was burning to ask. But there was no point since Lord Cecil had made clear this wasn't the time or place for their discussion. Besides, Lord Cecil's mouth was again stuffed to the brim, so he couldn't have answered if he'd tried.

She stared across to the plate she had pushed away, laden with white toast and two poached eggs. She slid it back towards her and took a bite, hearing Lord Cecil say in a muffled voice, "That's my girl. You need plenty of healthy food inside you for what's to come. You both do."

Robert leaned across the table and filled his plate a third time, taking more toast and jam.

***

As Naru's dreary and overcast sky loomed above, Lord Cecil resolved to spend the day exploring the bustling town market at the centre of Naru.

He deemed the market reasonably secure for the time being, believing that Lily's absence would likely go unnoticed in the Elders' realm for several days, and the bustling market would make it exceptionally difficult for anyone to single them out.

It's far safer than venturing into the open expanse or amidst the dense foliage, he mused.

Lord Cecil had opted to linger in the market for a few hours, intending to transition to the next port key at dusk when the crowds had thinned, allowing them to slip away discreetly.

The vibrant town of Naru offered a mesmerising display of diverse cultures coexisting in harmony, and the overcast weather was soon forgotten.

The streets hummed with a multilingual buzz as vendors from different lands sold their wares with a flurry of exotic accents.

Shops adorned with spellbinding sigils and mystical runes proudly displayed magical items of all shapes and sizes, inviting passersby to marvel at their enchanting wares.

Lily looked about, her senses evidently assailed by the cacophony of sights and sounds. She kept looking up at Lord Cecil, saying, "Wow, this is amazing!"

"It certainly is, Lily. It's a most marvellous place."

Lord Cecil was also watching Robert with a hint of amusement.

The young man seemed utterly out of his comfort zone, his posture stiff and his eyes wide as he scanned the bustling marketplace. It was obvious that Robert had never witnessed magic on this scale. The open displays of spells, fantastical creatures, and peculiar trinkets must have been overwhelming for someone raised amidst the strict limitations of the Elders' society.

Lord Cecil could practically see the swirl of apprehension in Robert's mind, a fear of the unknown, the ever-present worry of the Elders' magical police apprehending him for simply being there. Or perhaps it was a fear of his parents' potential disapproval.

A wry smile played on Lord Cecil's lips.

Gradually, as the minutes ticked by, the tension began to drain from Robert's posture. His shoulders relaxed, his gaze softening as he took in the sights and sounds.

Lord Cecil offered a warm smile, a silent reassurance to the young man. Robert, in turn, responded with a smile of his own, a flicker of curiosity seeming to replace the earlier apprehension. The wonder of the magical marketplace was slowly winning over his initial fear.

***

As Lily strolled past a group of students, she couldn't help but notice their vibrant robes and hefty stacks of books. The students' attire hinted at their affiliation with a nearby school that specialized in the arcane arts. Lily imagined what it would be like to be one of the students, lost in thought about the endless possibilities of a life in magic. This had long been her dream, and she couldn't believe such a magical place existed. She buzzed with excitement.

As they turned the corner, they saw a sign that read 'Willow's Wand Shop' tucked away in a small alcove, the store's windows filled with rows of intricately carved wands of all shapes, sizes and colours, each one unique in its design and properties. A faint blue mist seemed to emanate from the shop, giving off a pleasant smell that enticed the many passersby to come in.

For Lily, who had grown up in a world devoid of magic and wonder, Naru was a revelation. She felt a newfound sense of freedom and boundless curiosity, eager to learn everything she could about the world and its enchanting secrets. Even Robert was now getting swept up in the allure of the town, beginning to behave more bravely as his eyes darted around in wonder.

Lord Cecil, ever the vigilant strategist, warned them

of the dangers lurking amidst Naru's veneer of neutrality. "Remain alert and cautious at all times and always stay by my side."

As Lord Cecil issued his warning, a nagging sensation gnawed at the back of Lily's mind.

What does this Abaddon want with me?

Could this so-called prophecy be true?

What's going to happen if he finds me? Does he have plans to kill me? Or exploit me in some way? Anyway, why me? What's so special about me?

The questions seemed endless, all popping into Lily's head one after another. However, as quickly as they entered her mind, she found herself distracted.

At one stall, a friendly-looking wizard was selling a variety of potions and elixirs, each with its own unique properties.

Lily was fascinated by the colourful vials and bottles, and the wizard happily demonstrated their effects, pouring a small amount into a glass and swirling it before taking a sip himself. The potion turned his tongue blue and made him speak in a high-pitched voice.

Robert recoiled as if in terror at the spectacle, while Lily tilted her head back and burst into laughter. Robert looked agog at her, then joined in with the laughter.

Lily's laughter was so unrestrained that it transformed into a series of playful snorts, causing Robert to chuckle even harder, to the point where he said, "Lily, stop! My ribs are aching!"

She chuckled too, and all the while, out of the corner of her eye, she could see Lord Cecil watching with a slightly bemused expression, the way a mother cat looks at its naughty kittens.

"You two," said Lord Cecil in an amused tone, though he wasn't laughing, "I think you should tone it down. Everyone will think you're quite mad. Or at least too rambunctious."

"Sorry, Lord Cecil," Lily said. "We're sorry, aren't we, Robert?"

Robert looked up, solemnly nodding before promptly bursting into more giggles.

"We are supposed to keep a low profile, you know," urged Lord Cecil, leaning in towards the two of them. As he did so, they looked up with startled eyes.

Lily whispered, "I forgot …" From now on, she and Robert crept around like mice.

"You can still enjoy yourselves, you know," said the elder man. "Just don't go overboard."

Lily and Robert nodded.

As the trio ambled through the bustling streets, their nostrils were tantalised by the irresistible aromas of caramel and cinnamon infused with a dash of smoky heat emanating from a cart that beckoned to them. It boasted a sign reading 'Dragonfire Popcorn.' Lily, in particular, was captivated by the fragrance, and without a second thought, they approached the vendor.

With a jingle of coins, Lord Cecil procured two small brown paper bags, which the vendor filled to the brim with the undoubtedly fiery treat. The kernels themselves were a deep shade of red, hinting at the inferno of flavour to come. As Lily gingerly took a bite, she was greeted with an explosion of warmth in her mouth that soon permeated throughout her body.

"That's insane!" she said. "It's like having a roaring fire in my belly! But in a nice way."

How right she was! To her utter astonishment, small flames burst forth from her mouth as she spoke, and from Robert's, too. And they enjoyed breathing fire at each other.

"Look at me! I'm a dragon!" said Robert effusively.

Lily nudged him with her elbow. "Shh," she said. "Remember, we have to keep low key …"

Robert hushed, but now and then, he huffed out a dart of fire before sucking it back in.

As they made their way down through the bustling market, they passed by a street performer juggling glowing orbs that seemed to dance in the air, leaving behind trails of glittering sparks.

The performer's face was painted with intricate designs, and his movements were so fluid and graceful that it looked as though he was casting spells with each toss.

Farther down the market, a number of musicians were playing a lively tune on their instruments, their melodies blending with the uplifting tinkling of a nearby fountain.

Lily couldn't resist the urge to dance, and she grabbed Robert's hand, pulling him into the throng of people dancing and clapping along. "Lord Cecil!" cried Lily, having great fun. "Come and dance!" But Cecil just slightly bowed, a small smile gracing his lips.

"Thank you but no, not for now as I'd probably give myself a hernia."

Soon, Lily and Robert ceased their frolicking and rejoined him.

The trio then made their way over to a small wooden platform in the centre of the bustling market, and the bright sign above it caught the attention of many passersby.

A young man with a large bright blue wizard hat weaved in and out of the small crowd, coaxing them to drop coins into it.

Out of nowhere, a brightly coloured wizard appeared on the platform, adorned in a long blue robe with yellow stars and a long blue pointy hat. He almost tripped over his trailing attire, but quickly recovered and addressed the crowd with a booming voice. "Ladies and gentlemen, boys and girls, witches and wizards, sorcerers and sorceresses, *he* and *she's*, *they's* and *them's*, and all those in-betweens. I am Gadabout the Great!" He scanned the crowd with enthusiasm.

The wizard then turned to his young assistant with bated breath. "Did I miss anyone?"

The assistant wore a deadpan expression and replied with a low, gravelly voice, "Dunno."

Lily, Robert, and Lord Cecil looked on in bemusement but with eager curiosity, waiting for the performance to begin.

"Be prepared to be amazed!" the wizard announced. "For what I am about to perform is—"

"Oh, for goodness' sake, get on with it!" someone in the crowd shouted. "Haven't got all week!"

The wizard, slightly irritated, gritted his teeth and forced a smile.

"All right, all right. My wand, please!"

The young man, whose expression hadn't changed, retrieved a slender wand from beneath his long brown ragged jacket and passed it across to the wizard.

He took a melodramatic pose and waved the wand above his head, chanting a spell that instantly engulfed him in a puff of smoke.

His hair slightly frizzled, he declared confidently, "Ta-da! Magic. I am now invisible."

But someone in the crowd shouted out, "Well, that's funny because we can still see you."

The wizard looked on in confusion.

"Are you sure?"

Another voice shouted, "Yes!"

"And I can see you as well!" cried a third.

The wizard, as if not knowing quite what to do, started muttering to himself as the unimpressed small gathering started to stroll away.

"Wait, wait! I have other spells that will amaze, astound, and bewilder—" he pleaded with the crowd. But before he could even finish his sentence, he was struck with a flying vegetable that hit him square in the face. He teetered and tumbled off the rickety wooden stage, crash-landing onto the hapless assistant below, creating a spectacularly unsightly heap on the ground.

Lily and Robert looked on and giggled helplessly, while Lord Cecil gave a wry smile and quipped, "Well, that was certainly entertaining. Come on, let's go before he has another disaster."

As they continued to explore the market, Lord Cecil kept a watchful eye out for any signs of danger. His sharp senses and years of experience made him a valuable companion in this unpredictable world. Soon, they stopped at a meat stall, and Lord Cecil and Robert marvelled over the impressive displays of meats laid out before them. The two began to debate how many slices of meat to purchase, leaving Lily slightly irritated as she watched them bickering.

They're so ridiculous. How can they still be hungry after such a huge breakfast? Boys … they are greedy, impossible things!

Lily turned around, taking in the sights, smells, and sounds of the market as she did.

She found her attention drawn to a small tent a short distance away, nestled between two stalls. She felt strangely compelled to it, her feet moving of their own accord toward it, taking her farther away from Lord Cecil and Robert.

They didn't seem to notice her wandering off.

Lily sauntered towards the tent, the sounds of the market drowned out by silence.

Her entire body was being pulled towards the tent as if a magical rope happened to be drawing her in. Before she knew it, Lily had stepped over the threshold, quite entranced.

Inside the tent, the musty smell of old fabric and incense wafted into her nose, claiming her senses. She found its interior illuminated by a single tabletop candle, barely lighting the space, leaving most of it shrouded in shadows. A haggard old lady sat hunched there on a rickety chair.

Her eyes, a piercing blue glowing in the dark, flicked up to meet Lily's.

The wrinkles on the old lady's face were so deep they looked like the grooves on a weathered tree trunk; her hair, a wild mess of grey and white, hung around her shoulders in horribly unkempt strands, akin to a tangle of sodden hay on a terribly wet afternoon.

Lily could see the hag's clothes were threadbare, their fabric patched and mended many times.

The old lady peered up at Lily with such intensity that it seemed she could read her thoughts.

"Would you like me to read your fortune, girl?" the woman asked, giving a false smile.

"Hmm, okay then." Lily offered her delicate hand, not even sure why she'd do such a thing.

She swallowed hard, hesitantly taking a seat opposite the old lady at the small table.

"I believe in magic. But not fortunes," she whispered. "Or fate. I think everyone makes their own choices, silly or sensible." Lily spoke with conviction.

The old lady grinned, placing her rough palm over Lily's. "Oh, do you now, young one?"

"Y-yes," said Lily, stuttering. "I do."

The hag began to speak a rhyme, staring intently.

"Destiny's enchantment grips us tight, life's game being played with hidden might. Yet, within the labyrinthine way, through to the close of a preordained day, the wanderer must chart their course, carving their path to fate's ultimate force."

The old lady spoke the rhyme in a hushed voice, pulling out from a small bag a necklace with a sphere-shaped vial containing a beautiful blue liquid.

Lily was mesmerised by the sight of it.

"But I don't have any coins," she said, pouting.

If only she had some money of her own to give the woman.

The woman smiled again, holding out the necklace to her. "My gift to you, child. A drink of this will bring back the one at death's door. Use it wisely."

Lily's mind was ablaze with alarm as she pondered the identity and intentions of the mysterious elderly woman. Why would she offer her such a precious gift?

As the woman extended her hand, Lily couldn't ignore the rough, ridged texture of her skin, evoking images of ancient tree bark.

Despite her hesitations, Lily found herself reaching out and accepting the offering, promptly draping the necklace around her slender neck.

"That's so … It's so kind. I can't believe you would give me something so beautiful," she said in a soft voice, thanking the giver.

Captivated by the beauty of the object, Lily's suspicions drifted off.

She tenderly examined its craftsmanship with her fingertips, her hand running down the length and stared at the shimmering blue liquid within the sphere vial now tucked in her dress.

Out of nowhere, Lord Cecil and Robert burst abruptly into the tent.

"My goodness, Lily. What are you doing here? We have been searching for you. You know you can't just run off like that! Your life depends on it," Lord Cecil warned, his face red.

Lily snapped back into the moment as if she had been in a strange trance; she felt dazed, just as she had when she'd first woken up from her nightmare early this morning.

"I'm sorry," she muttered. "This nice lady was just going to read my fortune, and I felt it was quite harmless," she added in a small voice. "She gave me …"

Lily knew she should have mentioned the necklace adorning her neck, but her voice faltered when she attempted to do so. She didn't want to tell them. It felt like a private, personal gift.

"Someone gave you what? And what lady?" Robert quizzed.

"Here …" Lily gestured as she turned to her side.

There was nothing but an empty seat.

Lord Cecil and Robert shared a puzzled look, their eyes darting around the empty tent.

Lily rose to her feet, her slender fingers grasping the necklace around her neck.

It was still there, so she hadn't hallucinated, but how then did the woman disappear?

"We must go now," Lord Cecil ordered briskly, and Lily sensed the urgency in his voice.

"What's wrong?" She raised a quizzical eyebrow, her eyes darting from Lord Cecil to Robert.

Lord Cecil leaned in towards Lily's ear.

He whispered, "When we were searching for you, we overheard whispers in the market. We've been discovered already; they're looking for us, Lily, but I don't know how, or how it's happened quite this quickly. Regardless, there's no sense in wasting time trying to work it out as if it's a riddle. The fact is, it's too risky to stay; we must head out now to the next port key."

Lord Cecil's voice was filled with grave concern as he peeped from the tent warily.

"Come on."

The trio raced through the twisting, narrow corridors of the upper Naru market. With every step, they kept their heads low, darting through the bustling crowds.

Unease enveloped them; Lily and Lord Cecil were especially worried that at any moment, someone might recognise them, aware of the ongoing pursuit.

They hurriedly brushed past groups of rowdy youths and seasoned merchants peddling their goods, determinedly pushing forward towards their destination.

Suspicious glances from the marketgoers pierced them as

they rushed by. Now, it felt as though everyone around could be an enemy, that every piercing gaze was watching, reporting on where they were, where they headed, what they wore.

There was no room for complacency or rest, now feeling like fugitives.

The trio's pace quickened, and they slipped behind the market stalls and plunged down a dank, malodorous alleyway. The gravity of the situation finally dawned on Lily. She was being pursued by malevolent wizards, and the weight of that realisation filled her with dread.

Until now, it had been some vague notion in the back of her mind, not thinking that danger could be lurking around every corner.

Lord Cecil, too, struggled to keep up, his breaths coming heavily.

They maintained their brisk pace despite Lord Cecil battling to keep up. He could not feign that he was as fit as he used to be, having grown used to evenings of good and plentiful food, lots of rest and his fair share of alcoholic drinks; his paunch was a testament to fine living.

The alley went uphill, and as the trio made their way deeper into it, the atmosphere became dark, dingy and suffocating, making Lily's skin prickle with unease.

The dim lighting cast eerie shadows along the walls, and the sound of the trio's footsteps resounded off the rough-hewn stones. They passed two men, and Lily couldn't help but notice their ragged clothes and furtive glances. The parchments they were handing out seemed innocent enough, but Lily sensed something more behind their purpose.

The outline of a black swallow also drew Lily's attention like a magnet.

It was meticulously drawn on the parchment paper in black ink, the bird's wings outstretched in a graceful arch, its sharp beak pointed towards the sky.

A little farther down, a man stood on a wooden crate; he had wild, unkempt hair and eyes that burned with intense fervour. He yelled out words as if delivering a passionate sermon.

Most of what he said didn't make any sense, but he said one thing at least with relative clarity.

"Darkness gives rise, light falls, balance will restore."

The message was still cryptic and unsettling, leaving Lily to wonder, *are they just the ramblings of a madman or are we supposed to work out what he means?*

As they emerged from the alley, the weight of the eerie atmosphere lifted, and Lily could breathe again. They now found themselves on the uppermost hill of Naru.

***

A breathless and exhausted Lord Cecil pointed to a small chapel a few feet away, above them on top of the hill. "The port key is inside that chapel," he said panting, pointing ahead of them.

They strode briskly up the narrow, cobbled street, its stones worn smooth by centuries of footsteps. The ancient chapel loomed ever closer, its spire reaching towards the sky like a skeletal finger. But as they approached, Lord Cecil's unease grew, a gnawing feeling that they were not alone. He pretended to ignore it, quickening his pace, but the sensation persisted.

It was akin to an insistent nagging thought at the back of

his mind.

Finally succumbing to the mounting unease, he abruptly turned on his heels, his eyes darting across the empty street behind them. An initial sweep revealed nothing amiss, but keen instincts led him to discern the presence of two imposing figures shrouded in masks, skulking behind a brick wall. Their silhouettes melded seamlessly with the encroaching shadows.

Lord Cecil's mind raced, meticulously calculating potential outcomes.

Maintaining a façade of nonchalance, he pivoted back with a carefully neutral expression, feigning ignorance of the unfolding threat.

"Quickly! This way," Lord Cecil urgently pressed, his voice betraying strain as he pulled at Lily and Robert's arms, guiding them down another dim alleyway. Dodging left and right, they navigated the labyrinthine paths until they reached a flight of stairs ascending.

Without a moment's hesitation, they scrambled up the steps, breaths ragged until they burst through a sturdy wooden door, finding refuge in the cool, dim sanctuary of the chapel.

As Lord Cecil bolted the door behind them, he scanned the chapel, his eyes settling on a small wooden pillar in the farthest corner.

"Run there!" he shouted, his voice indicating urgency. "Hurry!" He watched Lily and Robert sprinting towards the pillar, their footsteps echoing through the cavernous space.

Lord Cecil bolted the door behind them, his eyes scanning the shadowy space.

Reaching the pillar, they found a concave bowl filled with

shimmering water.

Lord Cecil didn't waste a second. "Place both hands in the bowl now!"

Just then, the sound of splintering wood shattered the air as two masked men burst in, wands at the ready. With a swift motion, they unleashed bolts of electricity, crackling through the air towards the trio. The deafening blast boomed through the chapel, smoke and dust billowing.

The men squinted through the murk, searching for signs of their prey. As the haze cleared, the floor lay bare. Lord Cecil, Lily, and Robert had all vanished.

Chapter Four:
Blood Will Have Blood

Lord Walsingham walked hastily as he entered the hall of the privy council, joining the rest of the elders who were already all seated around the long table. He was the last to arrive, which was uncommon for the normally punctual Lord Walsingham. The large wooden door slammed shut behind him, the bang echoing through the large space as every eye fixed on him.

Lord Walsingham scanned the hall and finally found the only empty seat, easing himself into it as he now sat before the large oak table positioned at the centre of the hall.

Lord Walsingham took a minute to observe the fragile councillors sitting around the table, the tension simmering around him. The great fire roared at the hall's end, casting a flickering light that danced against the walls. Yet, despite its fervent flames, murk hung thick in the air, refusing to dissipate. Muted whispers and hushed tones flowed around him, a constant hum.

A few strides away, the High Councillor, Lothar, perched at the head of the table, flanked by a pair of wand-wielding guards standing sentinel in his defence.

Lothar's attention fixated on the assembly of councillors, scrutinising their subtle gestures and flickers in his direction. He swept the hall with his eyes, registering the council's unease.

With a sigh, he tapped his wooden gavel three times, demanding their focus.

The chamber fell silent as every eye pivoted towards

Lothar, anticipating the motive of the meeting. He scanned the assembly again before fixing his stare on Lord Walsingham.

"I presume, Lord Walsingham, that your charming daughter is yet to return after her ... unexpected departure?"

Lothar's tone implied he already knew the answer, but his motive was to agitate.

His bloodshot eyes glared at Lord Walsingham, exposing the malevolence behind his diminutive figure.

Lord Walsingham stared back, pausing to suppress the vexation brewing in him. A sense of impending danger coursed through his veins, causing the hairs on the back of his neck to rise.

"What concern is it of the council?" Lord Walsingham lifted his brow in response. "The whereabouts of my family are private, not a matter requiring a meeting. But I appreciate your *sincere* concern, gentlemen," he added, glancing around the chamber nonchalantly.

Lothar scoffed. "Concern, you say? I must admit, it was a cunning move to send the girl away with Lord Cecil, using an *unregistered* port key to transport her. And I wonder how you entrusted such an undertaking to that hapless, corpulent buffoon. However, that is all irrelevant now. I must insist that you hand the girl over to me immediately."

Lord Walsingham slouched back in his seat, his expression vacant.

"And for what purpose, may I ask?"

Lothar gave a forced grin as he locked his eyes on Lord Walsingham.

He said, "For her own safety, of course. No doubt you've heard the rumours. Her wellbeing is of the utmost importance to all of us in the city."

Lord Walsingham gave a defiant and sarcastic smile.

"Lily is perfectly safe wherever she is. There is nothing more to discuss."

Lothar studied Lord Walsingham's expression, his fingers tightening around his wooden hammer.

"Lord Walsingham," Lothar said. "You seem to forget that you're not only a member of this council, but also a citizen of this city. And as such, you have a duty to ensure the safety of its inhabitants. If your daughter is in danger, it's our responsibility to ensure her protection."

Lord Walsingham leaned forward, his eyes blazing.

"This has nothing to do with Lily!" he cried out.

"You and I both know it has everything to do with her. I demand that you hand her over to us immediately. The future of our great kingdom relies on that little girl!" Lothar yelled.

Lothar's dispassionate smile had turned barbaric, his patience running out as he burst into a sudden fit of rage, banging his fists against the oak table, startling the seated council members.

They began to murmur among themselves.

Lord Walsingham remained unfazed as he straightened in his seat, glaring at the slender figure of Lothar who now wore an unrecognisable expression, his eyes alight with fury.

Lord Walsingham paused, and with a measure of control, finally replied.

"I'm afraid I can't do that."

Lothar shook with rage, his own eyes on fire now.

"You dare challenge my authority? I'll have you arrested and tried for treason. Guards!" he roared sternly, sitting upright in his high seat, looking around for his guards.

The guards approached Lord Walsingham with a determined grimness, the heavy thud of their boots filling the hall as they closed in on him.

The rest of the council members sat frozen, too terrified to speak or act. Triumphantly, a smug grin took over Lothar's face as he watched the unfolding scene.

Once friends and allies, their relationship had soured into bitter rivalry over the years. Walsingham was popular among the people and respected among his fellow councillors. With him out of the way and the girl caught, Lothar's grip over the city of Elders would be complete.

Just as the guards were about to apprehend Lord Walsingham, the grand wooden doors of the Great Hall burst open with a thunderous crash.

The council members jumped in their seats, Lothar whirling in terror.

In he strode, a man draped in a long, tattered black cape and black garments beneath.

His long, shaggy brown locks cascaded around his face in unkempt waves, framing his sharp features, while piercing green eyes showed a fiery intensity reflecting a mighty and potent presence despite his thin frame.

A jagged scar snaked down the left side of his face, adding to the menacing appearance.

As he walked, he exuded dark mystery and intrigue, and those who saw him couldn't help but feel unsettled. Even the air around him seemed to be charged with a dangerous energy.

But he wasn't alone. Behind him lumbered a hulking and formidable creature, towering over seven feet tall. It was a Herne, a rare and mythical creature of warrior blood, known for its lupine facial features and formidable physical prowess, as well as for its skills of ancient sorcery.

The Herne was a true marvel of nature, with fur that shone like black obsidian, and eyes that gleamed with an intelligence almost human-like.

The colossal Herne towered over the assembled council, its piercing gaze fixated on their quivering countenances, sensing their terror. If it so desired, the Herne could slaughter each and every person in the chamber with its brawny hands and spine-chilling magical powers; this was a truth evident to every individual present, prompting them to tremble in its presence.

Lord Walsingham, however, remained unfazed and stoic.

"What is the meaning of this?" Lothar demanded, his voice quivering.

The shaggy-haired man strode forward, piercing green eyes locked onto Lothar with unwavering intensity as he walked up to Lothar's seat. He pulled out a long wand from the inside of his garments with his left hand, making a flickering gesture with it.

The two guards were instantly disarmed, frozen still, unsure of how to stop this stranger. They were equally stunned by the speed with which they had been parted from their wands.

The man stood before Lothar, hovering over him, laying his wand on his shoulder.

But his relatively gentle touch was not one of affection or respect. The man's icy green eyes revealed a deep disdain for Lothar as the high councillor feebly looked up at him.

"Who are you? And how did you enter my city?" Lothar questioned meekly.

"I was invited," he nonchalantly replied as he leaned towards Lothar, holding his gaze.

"How dare you! I control who comes in and out of my domain. I gave no such order!"

The man standing above peered down, pressing his wand harder into Lothar's upper body.

He spat out, "Do you feel in control now?"

Lothar stared back as if sensing the man's deadly intentions, stalling for time; perhaps he was hoping more guards would arrive to catch the perpetrator before he did anything worse to him.

He spat, "I must warn you that using magic within this kingdom is strictly prohibited. If you were to dare to … kill me with that wand, you wouldn't make it past the walls of this city. You would be hunted down and killed like an animal!"

The man gave a guileful smile. "Very well then, as you please."

He slowly placed his wand back into his garment and Lothar momentarily appeared to breathe out in relief. But not for long. The man pulled a small dagger from his harness.

Lothar had barely set eyes on the object before the man deftly slid it across Lothar's throat in one swift movement, a red arc of blood spewing forth across the table.

Lothar made a horrifying sound and grasped his neck in a helpless attempt.

A futile attempt, for Lothar's bright blood would not stop its fountain.

A vile crimson stain soaked into his collar as he fell back in his wooden chair, gasping violently for air.

Everyone stared on, white and aghast.

"Who needs adversaries when the true enemy lies within?" said the man as he turned to the council, casually wiping the blood off his dagger with his garment.

He returned the deadly blade to the small harness.

No one had dared to speak up except Lord Walsingham, who had now got to his feet. "It will have blood, they say. Blood will have blood."

The man looked over at Lord Walsingham, his expression blank.

He stared for more than a moment.

"Where is the girl?" the man quizzed, breaking the silence, taking a single step towards him.

Lord Walsingham locked eyes with the man, Lothar's horrifying gasps continuing to taint the atmosphere.

"She is travelling through the port keys."

Lord Walsingham grinned as the man stared.

"Well, your city is breached and will fall hours from now. I'd advise you to make your exit plans," he said and stormed out, the giant Herne trailing after him.

Blood was still trickling from poor Lothar's mouth. No longer was there a flume of bright red lifeblood arcing high. He had all but bled out, the walls and everything around bearing witness to their surfaces having been painted top to bottom with the redness of it. His face had grown almost as pallid as flour, and there could be no mistake that these were his last moments.

His eyes were unfocused, almost lifeless as his head dropped forward to his breastbone; he gave a dreadful final choking sound, collapsing face down into the tabletop.

Lord Walsingham stared for a moment at the scene, smelling the iron-rich stench.

Then he rushed from the hall, headed straight for his manor.

Chapter Five:
Into the Unknown

Robert stumbled from the portal first, tripping over himself and landing face down on the hard ground uncontrollably. Lily and the plump Lord Cecil followed suit, knocking the wind out of him as they tripped over little Robert and collapsed in a messy pile.

Lord Cecil's weight was crushing the life out of both of them.

He pushed himself to his feet, relieving them of his humongous burden. They helplessly panted and struggled to get up, totally winded, their breaths uneven.

"Where ... are we? I think I'm going to throw up," Robert said, his face turning ashen and his legs wobbling a little.

"No idea, but that was close," Lily exclaimed, relieved.

"Far too close," Lord Cecil agreed with a hint of concern. "Did I hurt you, dear boy?" he enquired as he eyed poor Robert.

Robert looked up in between heaving. "You squashed me."

"Well, let that teach you not to go first through the portal. Or if you do, then get out of the way, lad, or you will cause a nasty accident."

So much for Lord Cecil showing sympathy. Robert carried on throwing up, and Lily moved to check he was all right. "Did he really injure you? Did you get crushed?"

"No, not really. I just was scared that he might. I'll be okay in a minute."

Lily was immediately struck by the parched heat hanging oppressively in the atmosphere, as if it were a relentless predator eagerly stalking its prey. Its blistering intensity was in stark contrast to the temperate weather just experienced in Naru, and she could feel the sweat trickling down her back, even though they had only just arrived.

Lord Cecil, however, seemed unfazed by the oppressive air, quickly gathering his bearings, and gesturing for them to follow. They trailed after him, their feet kicking up tiny swirls of dust as they walked out of the narrow alley and into the open.

As they emerged into a town square, the full extent of their location was revealed.

The sun blazed down on them, dazzling in its unrelenting brilliance. Lily threw her hand up to shield her eyes, but she couldn't help peeking through the gaps between her fingers.

Where are we going now? she asked herself.

As the trio entered the market square, they were greeted by a desolate and barren environment. The buildings here appeared rough and primitive, fashioned from sun-dried bricks and sand, topped with thatched roofs fashioned from dried palm fronds.

The sparse population seemed to have little to offer, with only a few vendors selling their spartan wares in a dusty marketplace.

Beyond the market square lay a small dock beside a wide, shimmering river. Here, clear water glistened in the sunlight, inviting the trio to explore its refreshing depths.

With ease and fluency, Lord Cecil approached one of the market stalls and began to barter with the vendor, who had a rich, sun-kissed complexion and spoke in an unfamiliar language. After exchanging gold coins for plain brown shawls, the trio wrapped them tightly around their heads to shield themselves from the blistering sun and conceal their identities.

Following Lord Cecil's lead, they made their way towards the inviting river.

At the docks, Lord Cecil negotiated with a grizzled boatman, his unfamiliar words commanding the man, "Fetch us a boat. Small boat, large boat, it doesn't matter. I can pay."

After successfully bartering, he gave the boatman three gleaming gold coins.

The man promptly barked orders at a nearby sailor, who sprang into action, untying one of the small, docked sailboats. With a sweeping gesture, Lord Cecil beckoned Lily and Robert aboard.

"Right, you two; you'd better settle down as we have a full day on this here vessel."

"Where are we going?" Lily asked.

But no answer came. Anyway, she was tired and would not ask again; they'd find out soon enough. They stepped aboard, seating themselves on a long horizontal plank across the rear of the boat, facing forward. As they set sail, Lily felt a wave of unease wash over her, her forehead slick with sweat. Surely, she wasn't feeling seasick already. They had barely set off!

Or was it due to the relentless hot sun baking the tops of their heads? She had so many questions buzzing around in her head. *Where are we going, and why are we not hiding?*

"Are you all right?" Lord Cecil asked, evidently noting her discomfort.

Another more urgent question came to mind. "Um ... excuse me, but where is the lavatory?" Lily asked, her cheeks reddening with embarrassment.

"I'm afraid there isn't one on board. You'll have to make do with going over the side of the boat," Lord Cecil replied apologetically. "When in a different land, you have to adapt, Lily."

Lily's eyes widened in disbelief, but she knew there was nothing to be done about it. Adapt? How could she ever adapt to this? Wouldn't everyone turn to stare at her? How embarrassing!

The three of them were feeling the sway of the boat.

The older gentleman extended a weathered hand and passed a humble wooden crate brimming with sustenance to the younger man, who adroitly laid it down and commenced with fine-tuning the rigging, adjusting the ropes with precision to harness the caress of the gentle breeze.

Meanwhile, the elder fellow deftly employed a lengthy wooden pole to propel the craft farther into the watercourse, until the vessel was well and truly set to sail.

The boat steadily made its way towards the middle of the river, buoyed by the current, Lily's eyes wandering towards the far side where a lone figure perched on a canoe, wielding a spear to incite the fish into his waiting net. A group of children frolicked atop an overturned vessel nearby, while a cluster of women busied themselves with laundry down by the water's edge.

As the hours melted away, the day bled slowly but surely into nighttime, with the sun dipping below the horizon which was soon bursting into a dazzling display of celestial splendour.

Lily was spellbound, her gaze locked onto the distance in wonder. Never had she witnessed such a clear and vivid sky, where the stars were so plentiful that they seemed to spill out beyond the reaches of the universe. The sight was nothing short of amazing to her.

The young sailor, steadfast and tireless, paddled the boat deeper into the boundless river, charting an unwavering course ahead. Lily, lost in thought, stared down at the tranquil waters, her mind entranced by the gentle ripples the oars created, each dip and pull shimmering under the flicker of the moonlight. The voyage had been tranquil, with the water as smooth as glass, and the quietude only being broken by the lulling sounds of the waves.

Robert had drifted off to slumber, completed tired out, while Lord Cecil was still wide awake, his eyes fixed on Lily with a tender smile. Lily returned his expression, watching him for a bit.

Yet she also couldn't shake off the unease and the odd sense of hurtling towards something significant, something of which she was unaware, that could alter the course of their world.

Lord Cecil eased himself against the wooden bench to get himself comfortable.

"Although darkness can blanket the world, fear not, for where there is shadow, light is sure to follow," he intoned in a soothing voice, reciting a line from some literary work or other.

His words were calming and hypnotic, and a sense of peace washed over Lily as she listened.

She looked up at the night sky and gazed in wonder at the stars and the moon, the stars such tiny pinpricks of luminescence, seemingly insignificant against such a vast black expanse.

The vivid big moon hung low on the horizon, casting a

soft glow over the water and illuminating the ripples trailing behind the boat.

It was a serene and enchanting scene, and as Lily's eyelids drooped, a sense of calm descended and she drifted to sleep, comforted by the sway of the boat and Lord Cecil's reassuring presence.

Chapter Six:
Siege of the Elders City

As the grey clouds scudded across the darkening sky of the Elders' realm, their ominous presence seemed to foretell of an impending storm. As if from nowhere, a brilliant flash of light shot up to the heavens, illuminating the skyline of the city of Elders in a fiery glow.

The clouds above the city seemed to catch fire, their edges flickering like flames in the wind.

From every corner of the city, dark-cloaked figures materialised out of the shadows, as if summoned by the lightning bolt that had just struck. They moved in unison, converging on the city with a stealth and precision that spoke of years of training and discipline.

As they fanned out across the city, the cloaked figures made sure to cover every exit, ensuring that no one could escape their grasp. The silence that followed was only broken by the sound of the wind howling through the deserted streets, carrying with it a sense of impending doom.

The city was now surrounded, and its inhabitants were trapped like rats in a maze.

The sudden cries of, "We are under attack!" pierced the air, sending waves of panic through the city like ripples in a pond. A flurry of shrieks and shouts followed, the citizens of the city scrambling for safety. The streets below became a frenzy of chaos, window shutters slamming open, also the sound of shattering glass, people rushing from their homes by any means possible.

Through the darkness, masked figures moved through the streets like shadows, their footsteps ringing out on the cobblestones like thunder. Above them, plumes of fire jetted across the sky in different directions, like a twisted dance of destruction. The flames seemed to be everywhere at once, casting an ominous glow over the city and turning the night sky into a hellish inferno.

As the chaos unfolded, a deep, booming gong thundered throughout the city like a warning of the unthinkable. It was a sound that struck dread into the hearts of even the bravest citizens, a warning almost forming an attack of its own. Its foreboding reverberations seemed to shake the very foundations of the city as if signalling the beginning of the end.

Next, a deafening explosion rocked everything, rippling out in waves of destruction. The sound was so loud that it pulsated through every building, every street, every alleyway. Fumes billowed out from the epicentre, lightening the sky, illuminating the chaos below in a blinding glare. A tower shattered, the noise of its collapse mingling with the roar of the thunder that followed. It was a scene of utter devastation, the likes of which this place had never seen before.

The guards, sworn to protect the city of Elders, scurried through the city streets with their wands out, their faces set in expressions of grim determination.

As they ran, bolts of energy erupted from their wands, spiralling through the air in all directions like deadly serpents. The streets filled with the crackling of magic.

Body parts of the city guards lay strewn across the courtyard, copious arterial blood washing down the streets. The fight was brief and decisive, and there wasn't much saving to be done.

The city of Elders had fallen.

Lord Walsingham surveyed the damage, staring out over the city from the deck outside his bedroom loft. He felt utterly defenceless, devoid of any magical abilities; even if he'd had them, he was certain he would have stood no chance at all against these attackers.

He watched the smouldering fires here and there, eyeing the broken towers, the cracks in the temple dome, and many buildings fallen into great ruins. Inhaling deeply, he grappled with a rising anxiety that seemed to churn in the pit of his stomach. Nevertheless, as he evaluated the extent of the attack, the resultant damage appeared less extensive than he had imagined.

Lord Walsingham retraced his steps in his mind, having left nothing to chance. His dear Ursula was safely hidden away, despite her strong protests and pleas to remain by his side; he had done his duty, ensuring she was safe for now.

Lily was on the move with Lord Cecil and Robert, and Lord Walsingham had sent a message informing Lord Cecil of the Elders' city's devastating fall.

The enemy were closer to finding them; they needed to get farther away but he was unsure when, where, or even if Cecil would receive his message soon.

Now that the ancient magic no longer protected the city, Lily was in grave danger, and Lord Walsingham knew it was only a matter of a short time before the new occupiers would come knocking at his door, looking for her, accusing him of hiding her away.

What would they do to make him talk? He could not bear to even think about it, yet still, the many heinous thoughts invaded his mind regardless. They would torture him for sure, and they had so many ways in which to do it until he gave all her secrets away. The problem was, no matter what they might do to him, whatever grievous torture methods they might inflict, he could not produce the one they would come looking for. Because she was no longer here.

And that would only heighten the dangers for him since they'd say he was playing games.

Perhaps they will murder me, he thought. *I mean, why wouldn't they?*

He sighed and he paced, crossing the Great Hall a multitude of times in desperation as if willing himself to wear a hole in the already well-trodden ancient rug beneath his feet.

It didn't matter though, did it? Nothing mattered except for the safety of dear Lily and the boy, Robert. *Cecil will keep them safe,* he told himself. *Cecil knows what he's doing, and he's clever, and a good man, dependable and true.* That was the inner message his thoughts repeated to him by way of assurance, but the sad truth was that he did not even believe it. Yes, Lord Cecil was indeed a good man, and highly experienced. But the attackers would be just as good at their work, and there would be at least several of them. How could one man ever stand up to them?

So, none of this—not his thoughts, not his will or intent, and not his worries—could make a difference. There was nothing to tell them, nothing to assuage their anger, vitriol, and malice.

I could get the hell out of here, he considered momentarily. *If I left now, I could conceal myself in the great copse of trees across the way. I could take a horse, ride far ...*

Then, who am I kidding? No matter what, I am not about to abandon my city or fellow citizens. That is a preposterous and atrocious idea.

My job is to remain here, come what may. Let them come! Let them do their very worst.

I will not speak and at least they can be driven to the point of insanity, wondering what I hide.

Some of the city dwellers had fled, but just as many—likely more—had stayed with a view to not abandoning their homes and their little plots of land for which they had toiled so hard.

So, Lord Walsingham would stay, and he wasn't going to change his mind.

If he ran now, it was all over for the Elders' Kingdom.

He heard movements in the lower chambers of the house, fast approaching.

A little too early, aren't we? he thought, not moving a muscle.

He heard the creaking sound yet closer as the heavy boots climbed the stairs which led to the upper chamber where he was, the frightening sound getting closer and closer to it and to him.

He sucked in an enormous breath, the only real weapon he had on him—that of bravery.

Any moment now … May the Lord help me.

The noise of the boots stopped, and Lord Walsingham glared at the entrance, waiting as a loud, forceful knock at his door resonated through the chamber.

He took a deep breath and braced himself as the door flew open with such strength that it slammed back against the stone wall, the hinges breaking with a loud crack as it recoiled.

It fell slightly forward, loosely swinging, now dangling askew on one hinge.

Three figures barged in, their faces obscured by black masks covering eyes, nose and mouth.

Each intruder clutched a thick wooden baton, wielding it with what looked like a deadly precision, quickly closing in on Lord Walsingham. As they surrounded him, Walsingham quipped sarcastically, "Why the masks? Too afraid to show your—"

Before he could finish his sentence, he was struck on the back of his head, the immense force of the blow beyond brutal, sending him sprawling across the hard stone floor, face first.

Blood pooled around his head; his nose had been broken by the fall.

With every subsequent strike, the masked men relentlessly beat him with their batons, not caring if he was dead or alive for the beating. He was alive, hanging on to consciousness by what felt like the most tenuous sliver of reality. He no longer felt the blows, his mind willing death.

As they continued their savage attack, the room swirled and danced like a kaleidoscope as he battled his stubborn consciousness which, due to his fitness and relative youth, refused to die.

He could hear the masked men laughing and taunting him, their voices distorted by the blood pounding in his ears, the thump-thump of pulsing arterial blood all rushing to his brain.

If I cannot die, then I must fight back, he thought.

But his limbs were heavy, refusing to obey any command.

In between the blows and his battle for the survival he no longer craved, rational thoughts ebbed and flowed.

This makes no sense.

They will stop soon, he told himself, *because I am worth nothing to them dead, am I? They need information, and they can only extract that if they let me live.*

He had already committed to not speaking but who knew whether he would or not, under the circumstances? This was utter misery and torment, already a defeat of sorts to bring him so low.

As he lay there, helpless and in pain, he thought of his family, of the life he had built with Lily and Ursula. Suddenly, he was winded by a blow so powerful it made him cough up blood.

Abruptly, amidst the bedlam, a commanding voice sliced through the tumult, compelling the men to halt in their tracks.

Through his hazy vision, Walsingham could discern the odd silhouette.

I swear … my fractured mind plays tricks on me! his inner voice insisted.

He looked again. *No, no trick. He is really there.*

The shape of a diminutive goblin seemed to be standing above him.

The little masculine shape bore in its two hands a lengthy staff, crowned with a formidable stone that emanated a shadow, imposing and at odds with the being's minuscule stature.

"Pray, tell me, where is the girl?" inquired the figure with a cool composure that belied its size. Lord Walsingham endeavoured to stave off the encroaching haze of unconsciousness.

To be dead would be one thing, and right now, desirable. To be rendered unconscious was another matter entirely, a most terrible thought, a fate even worse than death.

Unconscious, they could do anything to him and when he again awoke, he would have to suffer through it over and over, drifting in and out of two horrendous states.

Despite the pain that wracked his body and the weakness threatening to overtake him, Lord Walsingham refused to back down. With every fibre of his being, he finally summoned up enough defiance to reply, his voice a hoarse whisper. "You will have to kill me first."

His eyes shone with fierceness, the depths of his soul laid bare in their gaze.

He was fighting for something greater than himself, something for which he would give his life several times over if he could, all of it without hesitation.

In that moment, he thought of Lily, the young girl he had come to love as his own daughter. He thought of her bright smile with those pretty pink lips, and of her tinkling laughter sufficient to brighten even the dullest of days.

He would do anything to protect her, even if it meant sacrificing himself.

The goblin still standing above him responded with a chilling glee, taking pleasure in his obnoxious tone. "There are far worse things than death, Lord Walsingham."

Chapter Seven:
Rhakotis

The fishing boat glided listlessly on the open waters as dawn crept through the clouds. Robert and Lord Cecil were still sleeping soundly, with Robert's head pressed into Lord Cecil's arm, his mouth dangling open as he drooled and snored.

Lily was slightly annoyed by the loud snoring, giving the boy a gentle kick on the leg.

Robert made a sudden loud grunt, and the snoring stopped. Absentmindedly, Lily played with the locket around her neck as she stared at the first streaks of light just beginning to appear in the eastern sky. The appeared silver, then pale peach, then scarlet as the glowing orb of the sun appeared at the horizon, dancing upon the surface of the water. The sky grew ever lighter, and a faint salty breeze lifted Lily's shawl, the sweet smell of the sea expanding her lungs.

"Rhacotis, Rhacotis!" the young man controlling the sailing boat said to Lily with a big grin, exposing the large gap in his front teeth. Lily almost felt tempted to smile. Lord Cecil and Robert were abruptly awoken too from their slumber at the gruff sound of the young man.

The city of Rhakotis sprawled out before them, a vibrant oasis amidst endless desert.

It was no makeshift tent city; this place was both solid and sizable.

The buildings were a mix of old and new, some bearing the signs of ancient architecture and others adorned with more recently built constructions.

The docks stretched along the river like a miniature town, low-lying buildings nestling alongside, connecting the docks to a nearly circular, decrepit wall part-encircling the city like a protective embrace. As they disembarked from the boat, the young sailor assisted them with cheerful energy before returning to his daily tasks.

Lily, Robert, and Lord Cecil gradually made their way beyond the city walls and into Rhakotis, traversing a narrow street flanked by towering sand-brick buildings.

They seemed to lean towards each other as if sharing secrets.

Bizarrely, once inside the beautifully crafted outer wall of such a solid and aesthetic design, the city appeared to assume no discernible shape or form; instead, the buildings haphazardly jostled for space along many twisting and turning streets.

They formed a labyrinth, and it was difficult to navigate.

Lily couldn't help but ponder how anyone could find their way around.

Still, they pressed farther into its depths, cautiously walking through the streets on the eastern end of the harbour, taking in everything going on. Discreetly, they wandered among the many stalls and the stores, and down into the narrow alley streets, trying to act nonchalant.

It was best if they attempted to look as though living there, which was not so simple when their meanderings meant frequently meeting dead ends and having to retrace their steps.

Lord Cecil urged, "I don't think we should stay here any longer than we have to. Let's get to the next port key straight away. What do you think, you two? Is that a good idea?"

He looked down at the two children's heads.

Now and then, he pointed in the direction he wanted Lily and Robert to follow, and they usually said nothing, trusting implicitly in him. If Lord Walsingham said Cecil was the safest person to be with, then who were they to question it? Regardless, he often asked, and listened.

Because of this, Lily looked up, smiled sweetly, and said, "Lord Cecil, it's so nice that you ask what we think but honestly, we'd follow you to the moon if you led us there."

"Yes," little Robert piped up, though he was quite breathless. "Let's just go where you want!"

Navigating the labyrinthine alleys, they emerged into a small town square, where Lord Cecil executed an intriguing gesture. His hand trailed along the top of a low, crumbling wall, gathering a handful of sand. Lily and Robert exchanged bemused glances, their curiosity piqued.

Before they could inquire about his peculiar action, they saw a woman wielding a small blade, leaning casually against a nearby wall. Both children knew this wasn't the time to ask anything.

There was little doubt that this woman was waiting there for someone or something. Sure enough, three other menacing figures hovered nearby, their gazes fixated on the visitors.

Advancing through the square at an accelerated speed, Lily, Robert and Cecil sensed an unsettling presence. The woman and—now—three men were keeping pace with great agility.

Forming a strategic semicircle, they brandished daggers, maintaining a calculated distance.

Lily looked up at Lord Cecil, her eyes wider than ever.

He looked down and gave a slight nod, a silent message. *Yes, don't you worry. I know they're there.* Lily trusted Lord Cecil to recognize how the situation would likely play out, and to deal with this quickly before things escalated beyond his capabilities to defend them all.

He leaned down sideways toward Lily, whispering.

"When I give the signal, I want you two to run as fast as you can and make your way up that alley ahead. Take a left turn and wait for me. If I don't return in just a few moments, then go and find the small oak door with a green ribbon on the outside. Enter, and stay inside."

The three men and the woman moved closer.

Lord Cecil spoke to them in a foreign language.

At first, they did not respond, and as he went silent, the woman pointed her knife at Lily and said something that sounded threatening. Lord Cecil responded gently, trying to calm the situation as he slowly reached for his pocket. The men became edgy, raising their knives.

Lord Cecil pulled out his money bag and stepped confidently forward, offering it to one of the men. The man stepped in closer too, his greedy hand extending to take the money purse.

As he did so, Lord Cecil threw the loose, dry sand from his other fist into the man's eyes.

"Run!" he yelled out.

Lily and Robert broke into a sprint, hurtling up the narrow alley, taking the first left turn as instructed. Then they waited nervously for Lord Cecil, hearing the loud grunts and shrieks of pain nearby. Lily's heart pulsed hard, worrying herself sick for Lord Cecil's safety.

"We have to go back!" Lily shouted, but Robert grabbed

her arm, stopping her from stepping outside unless she wanted the small boy to be seen dangling from her arm like a strange trinket.

"No. Just wait!" Robert insisted.

They both stood there, unsure of what to do. They waited anxiously.

After what felt like forever, they heard footsteps coming up the alley. Lily picked up a nearby rock off the ground, holding it high in a defensive position. She had never felt so ready to defend not only herself, but also the two she wanted to protect. She'd throw that rock so hard!

The tension was unbearable, and she feared the worst, but was determined.

As she got ready to strike, Lord Cecil emerged around the corner, placing something back inside his voluminous brown jacket.

Relief washed over Lily's and Robert's faces to see him unharmed.

"What happened to them?" Robert asked.

"Don't worry about them, boy. We need to keep moving. It's not safe."

Lord Cecil glanced around his surroundings again before beckoning Lily and Robert to follow him through another slim alley.

After a few minutes of walking, he finally stopped before a large wooden door with a small green ribbon tied to its round metal doorknob, just as he had described to Lily and Robert earlier.

He pulled open the wooden door swiftly, and Lily's mouth gaped at the sight of what lay before them. The hallway was empty, without a single soul. It looked abandoned, as if hundreds of years had passed and not a soul had ever walked inside.

The entryway to the building was particularly narrow and constricting, a challenge for Cecil.

No wonder no one had ventured inside and decided to stay!

The space could only accommodate one adult at a time with ease, though three could maybe squash in. Well, if anyone were to try to attack them here, they would have to enter one at a time, or risk getting stuck, which would make taking them on much easier.

Unless their would-be attacker were to be especially stick thin, of course. But even then, at least they would know he was coming; there was no way to just sneak up on them here.

Lord Cecil, in his usual manner, tried to lead the way, and they followed.

Lily's brow furrowed when he halted abruptly before even getting to the door. "Ah," he said. "Well, dammit. Unfortunately, you two may have to help me quite a bit," he said as he stared daggers at the doorway with its big thick supporting posts either side, and then the narrow passageway leading off from it.

Lily and Robert looked at him, confused. "Help you with what?" asked Lily.

"Well, it's been a while since …" Lord Cecil huffed and puffed, turning his great gut sideways, and still, it did not want to pass through the constricted passage. "You know, it's a while since I've been here. I must have put on a couple of pounds."

They looked him up and down, then eyed the width of the door. Hmm, awkward.

"Push my belly in through the door," he commanded. "Both of you; give it a good go."

He tried repeatedly on his own at first, dragging his back along the wall as he walked sideways, the passageway clamping around his portly frame and refusing to let go.

Lily worried if Lord Cecil would ever be able to squeeze through.

What if he gets stuck? she thought. *Then we're all trapped because he's blocking the way.*

He said more urgently, "I said push me. Push me! Use some strength!"

"But we'll hurt you," Lily protested, gently trying to ease his fat gut past the obstructing and projecting stones that jutted from the inner wall now and then.

"Push me! Harder! Give me a hefty, almighty shove!"

Lord Cecil again tried shoving his own girth through the narrow gap, but it was an awkward position. He took a deep breath and stretched his arms high to draw his solid stomach in.

Then all of a sudden, he disappeared through, like a cork exploding from the neck of a bottle.

Lily and then Robert followed, chuckling, though still apprehensive.

Inside, the passage was narrow at first, before opening into a large and wide courtyard, an utter surprise after all that squeezing and pushing. A gurgling fountain with wonderfully fresh spring water sat in the middle of the courtyard, providing a soothing, melodic sound.

Lily felt her unease dissipate as she walked past the fountain, inhaling the fresh, clean air.

"No one will ever find us here, Lord Cecil," she said. "It's a secret place. Like something from a fairy tale."

"Yes, well … we'll see," he responded, not instilling much confidence. "Suppose it'll do."

They crossed a massive, crumbling wall like the ones that surrounded the city. Intricate swirls, slashes, and stylised squares were carved into it, forming mysterious words a little like runes.

Lily did not understand them, but the symbols fascinated her, nonetheless.

As they continued on around a corner, Lily almost jumped sky high when they encountered an old man with stern, icy-blue eyes. He was just sitting there, on a stone ledge.

He greeted them with a nod, his gaze settling on Lily for a moment.

He seemed harmless enough, his weathered face showing signs of a life filled with experiences, and his dark skin appeared as if it had been forged in the fires of the sun.

Deep wrinkles surrounded his eyes, carved there like ancient hieroglyphics.

He wore a cloak of white and brown, clean and well maintained, in stark contrast to his surroundings. The man spoke with a deep and resonant voice, and while Lily couldn't comprehend anything of his message, it had a way of sinking into her chest like some sort of curious burrowing creature. She felt both fascination and uncertainty, standing staring at him.

The stranger just stared back as if it were a contest.

No idea what it was that he said, she thought. *Very enigmatic sounding.*

He pointed towards a wooden door, to which Lord Cecil

led them.

As they entered the dimly lit room, the man shut the door behind them, causing Lily and Robert to turn and look back at it, their expressions anxious. Lord Cecil remained calm, walking towards a small wooden table in the far corner as if familiar with the place.

The table was strewn with various everyday objects, including a rusted compass, a feather quill, and a leather-bound journal with frayed yellowed pages.

Lord Cecil examined the items carefully before lifting what appeared to be a brass teapot and placing it on a small, square-shaped stone table in the centre of the room. It had an air of antiquity like the passageway, as if preserved for centuries, unchanged by the passage of time.

Lily's mind buzzed with questions, and she couldn't wait any longer for answers.

She pleaded, "Please, before we continue. What compelled those people to chase us? Who were they, and why did that woman have her sights on me? And I also wanted to ask, why would Lord Walsingham send us into a magical world without any magic to keep us safe? I know you said this might not be the best time, but can't you tell me? It's all a bit … creepy!"

"Those individuals we encountered," Lord Cecil began gravely. "They're desperate to earn Abbadon's favour. They're mercenaries motivated solely by profit, devoid of any moral compass. For the right price, they'll carry out Abbadon's every command, no matter how sinister or dark."

As he spoke, Lord Cecil dramatically revealed a concealed wand from within his jacket.

Lily and Robert jumped at the sight. "You possess magic?"

Lily asked, screwing up her eyes as if she did not believe what she'd heard.

Lord Cecil nodded, nostalgia in his eyes.

"Indeed, dear Lily. I once served as a guardian, one of the select few entrusted with the Elders' city's protection. However, that was a bygone era. You see, we are obliged to retire at the age of forty, and the privilege of wielding magic lies exclusively with the guardians of the Elders."

He winked at Lily playfully, and she couldn't help but feel shock and admiration. "But why keep this a secret?"

Lord Cecil's response was sincere. "It never seemed pertinent, Lily. My primary concern has always been your safety."

Lily stood still, grappling with her astonishment.

The realisation that Lord Cecil had concealed such a remarkable ability from her for so long left her feeling foolish. "You know," he continued with a sly smile, "didn't you ever find it curious that at the ruins where you practised magic, you would consistently stumble upon rare and incredibly hard-to-find spell ingredients just a stone's throw away?"

Lily, nodded, embarrassed. "It was kinda weird, yes!"

She had often attributed those fortuitous finds to sheer luck.

In hindsight, the truth was obvious.

Lord Cecil smiled at the two, putting them at ease. "You know the drill," he said.

All three placed their hands on the brass teapot at the same time, feeling the warmth of its metal against their skin, and bracing themselves for whatever lay ahead.

Chapter Eight:

The Abandoned City

The Stygian-dark clouds that hung oppressively in the sky seemed to writhe and squirm with menace. Lily, Robert, and Lord Cecil emerged from the portal with a blinding, glimmering green light that flashed and pulsed for just a moment. Lily sighed in relief at being transported to a different place, but her relief was short-lived. This was all so dangerous!

Despair and guilt washed over her.

She was putting other people in danger, just to save her own life.

It's all very kind of them, she told herself, *but why me? Am I even worth it? What makes my life so important, and what if someone gets hurt? I'll feel terrible for all the rest of my days!*

As Lily looked around, she became even more anxious. They had arrived at the side of a road that ran through a desolate landscape with withered fields, and in the distance lay the ruins of several tall buildings. She looked up at Lord Cecil, her mind working overtime.

"The abandoned city. A permanent reminder of the scars of war," Lord Cecil muttered as if reading her mind. The ruins loomed like ghostly sentinels, with their jagged edges and crumbling façades an eerie reminder of the hideous and never-ending destruction wrought by war.

"We'll make our move to the abandoned city and on to the next port key," he added.

Lily and Robert nodded, Lily again hoping that their journey would be trouble-free. But the thought of spending any more time in this desolate wasteland made her skin crawl.

She couldn't wait to move on to the next port key, far from this haunted place.

As they walked towards the abandoned city, A peculiar breeze swept through, stirring the air before giving way to an eerie, unsettling calm. Lily shivered as the oppressive emptiness settled around them, and she couldn't shake the feeling that they were stepping into a realm of death and decay.

The scenery was lifeless, stripped of all vitality and hope.

Even the miserable clouds overhead cast a portentous shadow over that desolate terrain.

They ventured deeper into the city, the wind howling around them like a mournful symphony, swirling around the abandoned edifices like a choir of ghosts.

Two decrepit wooden chairs sat unoccupied, a poignant reminder of the lives once flourishing in this godforsaken place. The creaking of rusted metal and the hollow thud of their footsteps crunching on the rubble-strewn ground were the only sounds resonating. The silence was oppressive too, punctuated only by the occasional eerie moaning of the wind.

The shadows flickering around them seemed to whisper secrets of horror and despair.

"This whole place feels scary," Lily said, taking hesitant steps. "Don't you think? Like a place where ghosts live, and they come out and—"

"Lily, shut up. I don't like it either. It feels so spooky and deserted," Robert agreed, taking her hand for comfort. "But let's not talk about it, okay? I'm scared enough."

Lily silently agreed, holding on to his hand tightly, reminded of happier times when they'd played hide and seek in the ruins. "Things used to be so much easier here, Robert. Like … it seems a million miles away now, the life we used to have. Do you remember?"

He looked up and met her gaze, slowly nodding.

"Of course I do. I'll never forget, he said. "But we'll be all right."

"I hope so," Lily muttered, squeezing his palm tightly as they walked together like a girl and her little brother, one she was supposed to protect and care for …

Right now, Robert seemed to be the one protecting her instead.

The landscape around them seemed to press in, the silence suffocating in its intensity. Suddenly, the stillness was shattered by a high-pitched wail that made Lily's ears ring.

She instinctively covered them with her hands.

Lord Cecil pulled a small glass globe from his coat pocket, and it flashed with blue and orange light, illuminating Lord Cecil's face in a macabre glow. The high-pitched wail stopped.

An unfamiliar panicked voice echoed from within the globe.

Lily's blood ran cold, hearing the vile words.

"The Elders' Kingdom has fallen!" the little but tormented voice cried out in despair.

Lily could feel the weight of the words, the significance of the loss hitting her hard like a physical blow. The glass globe buzzed and then immediately fell silent and lifeless in Lord Cecil's grasp. They all shared a frightened look, the gravity of the situation sinking in.

Lord Cecil's expression was grim.

"We must hurry," he said, unable to hide how unsettled he

was.

As if on cue, the shadows that flickered around them began to take form. Masked figures in black robes stepped out from the darkness, their eyes gleaming with malice.

They were surrounded, with no way out.

A sudden flash of intense red light flew just above Lily's head, followed by an explosion.

The wall beside them toppled into a heap, sending debris flying in all directions. Smoke curled from the ruins, permeating the air with a thick haze.

Lily coughed and blinked furiously, trying to clear her vision which stung as if fragments of glass had embedded themselves in each eye.

Another lightning bolt whistled past, only missing Robert by a small margin. The heat seared Lily's skin as it streaked past her too. *We'll have to move fast to get out of here alive.*

"Run!" a voice thundered through the chaos, coated in trepidation.

Lily wasn't even sure who had spoken, but she felt her legs move as the three of them ran with all they had. More lightning bolts flew overhead, the masked figures trailing after them, wands in hand. Lily felt Robert's hand slip away from her grip, but she couldn't stop running to look back.

She ducked her head several times to avoid the flying sparks that followed her endlessly.

Her lungs were on fire, burning in the simple effort of breathing, her legs aching at each step.

But they just couldn't stop, not until they were safe.

She just kept running blindly through the dust and smoke, which made it nearly impossible to navigate her steps. She momentarily raised her head. Where were Lord Cecil and Robert?

She had lost them both, her gut churning, filled with dread. She had to toss the feeling aside. So, she scurried down a small alley up ahead and stood still there, frantically looking around for Lord Cecil and Robert. *I can't see them anywhere. God, please don't let me have lost them!*

Her eyes made out the shape of two silhouettes moving towards her.

To her terror, these were not the ones she wished to see. No, they were two masked figures moving like shadows in the night, their cloaks billowing behind them.

She froze in terror as she saw them. And the problem was, they had seen her too.

Without a word, the figures raised their wands, unleashing an orange ball of lightning that crackled through the air, hurtling towards the girl with deadly force.

In that split second, Lily's instincts took over. She ducked just in time, narrowly avoiding the incoming bolts that sent the walls crashing down around her.

The air was filled with dust and debris, Lily battling to catch her breath as she staggered to her feet, her eyes darting around frantically. *I can't get out! Help me! I can't find the way out!*

She prayed to Lord Cecil as if he could hear her by magic, and to Robert who always seemed to sense what she was thinking. And she prayed to the Lord in heaven that he heard her and took pity. Right at this moment, she would have prayed to anyone and everyone, so desperate was she.

Lily frantically turned the corner, her breaths coming in short, ragged gasps as she fought to keep her legs moving, her focus darting around for any possible escape route.

The man in all black stepped into her path.

Her eyes widened in terror as she took in the sight of the sleek-furred black creature beside him, its colossal size and features reminding her of the nightmares haunting her sleep.

For a moment, Lily was frozen in place, her mind struggling to process the danger, the horror.

But somehow, she found the courage to move, setting off running like a whirlwind, the terror that had gripped her seeping into her bones, filling her with helplessness and despair.

If she didn't find a way out soon, she would be doomed to die in this terrible, disgusting place.

But then, out of the corner of her eye, she caught sight of a narrow passageway leading off the main street. She threw herself into the opening, her body contorting as she crawled through the tight space as if potholing. Her fingers scraped against the rough-hewn brick and her clothes snagged on jagged edges, but she pushed on, determined to escape.

Finally, after what felt like an eternity, Lily found herself emerging onto a wider street, her eyes scanning the array of dilapidated buildings for any sign of safety. And then, she spotted it: a crumbling stone staircase leading up to the second floor of a nearby building.

She raced towards the stairs, her feet pounding against the rough stone.

But as she neared the top, she spied the rickety door that was off its hinges, swinging back and forth. For a moment, she hesitated, her mind racing. What might be waiting inside?

But then, with a deep breath, Lily stepped in, finding the cramped room dark and musty, the air thick with the scent of rotting wood and damp, fungus-infected stone.

But despite its dilapidated state, it offered at least a glimmer of hope.

Some of the walls had crumbled.

The roof, too, had eroded long ago, and the plentiful past rain had done its damage to the rest of the structure. Many holes dotted the floor, which looked fragile and smelled of rot and decay.

On the opposite side of the room, through a broken window, a rooftop connected to a big hall-like building. Lily panted, trying to catch her breath as she peeked around the doorway.

Had she lost them?

She looked down. He was there, the man dressed in black and the revolting large creature galloping at his side, both of them heading towards her hiding place. She panicked.

"Up there!" the creature grunted, informing the man in black.

"This is no good, they won't stop," Lily muttered to herself. Determined, she climbed through the window onto the roof, moving quickly along a row of precarious tiles. She stood shakily.

Some of the tiles worked loose under her feet, sending her into a dangerous skid.

Her arms flailed as she teetered on the edge, the yawning chasm below promising a fatal drop. With a desperate lunge, she managed to regain her balance and continue up.

Lily looked down, the ground far off, barely visible in the darkness. She jumped down a few feet onto a small balcony, her breaths coming hard, in stuttering gasps.

As she looked back along the roof, she spotted the man

in black with the terrifying creature as they arrived at the window. Fear spurred her into action, and she began to run again.

"Stop! Come back!" one of them yelled, but Lily kept moving, her heart thudding.

No, she wasn't going to let them have her. She worried about her innocent best friend momentarily. Where was he?

A ray of light shone out ahead, allowing a sliver of hope for an exit.

Lily found an open door and made her way through into the building, going down a large crumbling staircase into an entrance hall. Several narrow hallways were adjoined to the entrance hall, pointing in different directions. Unsure which to take, she ran down a large hallway to the right of the stairs. It was getting darker and much more difficult to navigate in the blackness.

And still she ran, stumbling into increasing darkness, each step fraught with uncertainty.

Shadows coalesced into wispy figures, appearing stealthily behind and beside her.

Her legs churned, propelling her through the hallway at a relentless pace. Bursting through a towering archway, she entered a large hall with its towering marble pillars.

Footsteps echoed ominously behind her, growing louder by the second. Desperation fuelled her feet as she dashed towards the hall's centre, searching for the exit that eluded her grasp.

What should I do? she wondered, helpless and overwhelmed.

In an instant, black-robed figures materialised from thin air, their faces hidden behind those sinister masks. They emerged from every corner of the expansive hall to form a ring around her.

It seemed to tighten with every passing moment.

As the figures encroached, Lily stood paralyzed.

Their numbers swelled, trapping her within their menacing circle.

Her escape routes had been sealed, as had her terrible fate.

The man in black—the one Lily had glimpsed earlier at the window, alongside the terrifying beast—charged into the hall, his presence commanding attention. Lily's eyes met his, a shiver jolting down her spine. She briefly looked into his blazing green eyes, every sinew afraid.

He had a jagged scar that ran down his left cheek, and despite his wiry frame, he exuded power and purpose, his visage twisting into that of a wild animal ready to strike.

Lily could only retreat, taking slow steps backwards until her back met the wall, sensing that death was looming.

As he raised his wand towards her, there was a deafening bang, a blinding burst of white light, and Lily crumpled to the ground with tremendous force, her body convulsing.

She was unable to move or control her limbs, left to lie there helplessly, vulnerable to whatever fate awaited her.

***

Robert and Lord Cecil ran into an alley, finally pausing to catch their breath. They had somehow managed to lose the masked figures.

Now, no longer running for their lives, Robert thought of Lily.

Where is she?

"We have to find her!" Robert exclaimed, increasingly agitated. "I let go of her hand," he mumbled to himself. "It's all my fault!"

Lord Cecil grabbed Robert by the arms, calming him down as he held the gaze of the child who had tears in his eyes. "First, it is no way your fault. And second, we must find somewhere to hide. Do you hear me? Now is not the time to start falling apart with *what ifs.*"

"No! I can't go on without her!" the boy screamed, not even caring who heard. "They'll kill her while we're hiding. I won't let her die!" Robert pleaded passionately, his cheeks bearing salty tracks. "Is it all my fault because I followed you?" His voice was thin, a wail escaping his throat, unable to talk properly anymore. "I wasn't supposed to come, and now see what's happened!"

His voice cracked again, becoming sobs, and his cheeks were red and mottled.

Lord Cecil looked at the poor child, placing his palms on each side of his face.

He stared into the boy's fearful eyes. "Look, I already told you, Robert. I know you care about her, but it's not your fault. Blaming yourself solves nothing. The best thing we can do to respect Lily is to put effort into escaping, all right? Lily wouldn't want you giving up, would she?"

He gently shook the boy by his shoulders. "Come on now. We have a job to do."

"But—" interjected Robert.

"You promised to do as I say, and now I'm telling you. We are no use at all to Lily if we're dead, are we? So, I need you to trust me, Robert. Lily is a clever girl; mark my words, she's probably hiding somewhere as we speak, and I suggest we do the same."

As Lord Cecil finished speaking, Robert's eyes drifted away, catching from the corner of his vision the horrible sight of a dreadful-looking creature lurking in the shadows.

The giant creature stood just a few feet behind Lord Cecil.

Robert recoiled visibly.

Lord Cecil reacted swiftly, putting his arm in front of Robert and pulling out his wand with his free hand, prepared to strike as he turned. His movement was quicker than his large frame would indicate, but the creature appeared even faster, grabbing Lord Cecil's arm effortlessly.

Why didn't Lord Cecil pull away?

"It's you!" Lord Cecil exclaimed, his voice tinged with relief.

The creature, so hideously towering and fearsome just moments ago, released Lord Cecil's arm abruptly, its grip loosening as if recognising a familiar face.

"Pies and age have made you slow, Lord Cecil," the voice proclaimed.

The figure grinned fiercely as he towered over Lord Cecil and Robert.

Lord Cecil scoffed slightly. There was only one thing to say. "Lily … You've seen her?"

The giant creature nodded. "If you want to see the girl again, I suggest you follow me."

"You know this … *thing?*" Robert began in an unmistakably frightened tone.

"Yes. This is Argog. I'm afraid there's no time for introductions or explanations, but I promise to tell you about him later," Lord Cecil said.

He then turned to Argog. "Go on then. Lead the way!"

***

The silence and stillness that had consumed Lily were shattered by the distant sound of wands being fired. Tormenting cries sliced through the air, leaving behind a lingering sense of dread.

Gradually, the numbness that had taken over her body began to wear off, and she struggled to pull herself onto her side before dragging herself up into a sitting position.

As her vision cleared, Lily saw a group of masked figures clad in black robes locked in deadly battle with a man who stood out from the rest. Dressed in his own tattered black robe, he moved with a fluidity that was almost graceful, exuding an air of confidence.

Is he a dark wizard? Lily wondered.

Lily remained rooted to the spot, unable to tear her eyes away from the bloody violence unfolding. Questions swirled in her mind.

Why is this dark wizard fighting the others?

Is he trying to protect me? It makes no sense! Doesn't he want me dead?

A bolt of bright red light narrowly missed the dark wizard. He whipped his head around, their eyes meeting for the briefest moment before he turned back to his opponents.

The sound of wands being fired grew louder and more frequent, and Lily had to escape before it was too late. As she tried to stand, the dark wizard noticed her movement.

With a flick of his wand, he sent her flying back, dragging her along the cold floor before thrusting her back against the wall, where she collapsed onto the frigid earth.

The dark wizard started chanting in a foreign language, a peculiar bubble forming around Lily. She pressed her fingers to the translucent shield now enclosing her, watching in amazement as one of the masked figures aimed his wand and fired a bolt of lightning at the bubble.

The bolt struck the shield but was deflected, hitting another masked figure.

It instantly crumpled, lifeless.

The masked figures had now entirely turned their attention towards the dark one, who smirked and raised his wand, assuming a fighting stance as they charged him.

The air crackled with a barrage of dazzling colours, shafts of blue and orange lightning bolts whizzing around the Great Hall. The masked figures were rapidly dwindling in numbers, unable to keep up with the relentless ricocheting power issuing forth from the dark wizard's wand.

The constant barrage lit up the hall, leaving pockmarks on its vast walls and sending chunks of plaster raining down on some of the attackers.

But still, they kept coming, pouring in high numbers as they relentlessly pushed forward.

Amidst the chaos, Lily sat stunned into immobility, rigidly holding her focus as beams of magic flew from every direction. Her eyes were fixated on the dark wizard, who expertly deflected every lightning bolt that came his way. It was like watching a god in action.

Lily wondered if he would continue to thrive or was getting close to his limits.

Nonetheless, he moved with ease, sending yet more balls of fire at the masked figures.

With a calm expression, the dark wizard stepped back and began whispering in ancient tongues, stretching out his wand before his face. A chain of unyielding, luminous orange fire streamed out of his wand, spurning, twisting, turning, hissing until it violently hurled itself around the hall. The spiralling fire struck and killed at least half of the masked figures instantly, leaving the air thick with the acrid smell of pungent burning flesh.

Undeterred by the gruesome scene, the dark wizard reached into his black jacket pocket and set loose a dozen paper swallows that soared above, hovering and circling the hall.

The lightning bolts continued to fly, but as Lily looked up, she saw the small paper birds diving into the masked figures, killing those they hit. It was a most peculiar, unfathomable sight, seeing such delicate, papery creatures causing so much dreadful destruction, and so easily.

Only a few masked figures remained, but their relentless attack on the dark wizard grew even more fierce and chaotic. And now, their combined efforts were paying off. A fortuitous twin lightning bolt bounced off a marble pillar and struck the dark wizard in the abdomen.

Lily watched nervously as he struggled to maintain his ground against the onslaught of attacks. But the masked figures were too many, and far too strong.

Another bolt of lightning hit the dark wizard, then another, until the last one winded him and he fell to his knees, coughing and spitting out blood.

As the dark wizard weakened, the protective bubble around Lily began to fade, her hope dwindling. She looked on as the man glanced briefly at her before mumbling something weakly under his breath. They were closing in on him.

"Argog, come," he muttered.

***

Argog, Lord Cecil, and Robert hastily made their way through the deserted streets.

A group of masked figures appeared from around the corner, blocking their path. Argog skidded to a halt, his eyes narrowing as he prepared to defend his companions. He raised his wand, electricity crackling along its length.

Without hesitation, he unleashed a barrage of lightning bolts from his wand, targeting the group, sending them flying backwards and clearing a path for them to continue. The air was filled with burned flesh and ozone, the masked figures lying motionless on the ground.

As they moved quickly through the darkened streets, Argog stopped dead in his tracks for a moment, as if listening to a whisper in the air. His eyes widened with great concern, and he grabbed both Lord Cecil and Robert, pulling them into his arms.

"No time! We must move quickly!" Argog shouted as he broke into a sprint, running as fast as he could, his dumbfounded companions being carried in his massive arms.

The world around them became a blur as they hurtled through the barren alleyways, the wind whipping through their hair. Lord Cecil and Robert clung on to Argog for dear life.

***

Despite the severity of his injuries, the dark wizard continued to duel down on his knees, determined. Lily watched in awe as he deflected every spell thrown his way, his wand movements almost too quick to follow. But as the protective bubble surrounding her dissipated, Lily realised he wasn't going to win. One of the masked figures had spotted her, pointing his wand in her direction. She knew to brace herself for the worst.

But before the figure could utter a curse, the dark wizard caught on, beginning to chant a spell of his own. A brilliant blue light burst forth, striking the veiled figure with such force that he fell to the ground in an instant lifeless heap.

Now, only one masked figure remained, and he and the dark wizard—still down on his knees, almost as if praying—faced each other, their wands at the ready.

Lily held her breath.

They shouted spells and sent lightning bolts hurtling towards each other. The bolts collided, the sounds of their impact deafening. But the dark wizard's lightning grew progressively stronger with each passing moment, overwhelming the other until he too fell to the ground, lifeless.

The hall fell into a deafening silence, interrupted only by the fluttering from a single paper swallow that hovered around Lily as if protecting her, also surveying the hall for danger.

A trail of blood and bodies littered the floor of the hall in every direction.

Lily looked around in horror, but her attention was very soon drawn to another soft sound in the hall. They were the strained and plaintive tones of painful pleas coming from the dark wizard, who had now collapsed to the floor, his body weak and damaged.

Lily walked quietly and cautiously towards him, stumbling through the bloody bodies to get to where he had fallen. She found him lying prostrate on his back in the middle of the hall, with his eyes fixed toward the high ceiling. His breathing was shallow, and Lily swallowed hard as she moved closer, crouching before the stranger who had saved her life.

She stooped, gazing at the man's face, taking in the details that had escaped her notice before.

She saw how there was a jagged scar running along his left cheek, an unmistakable mark of a violent past. His black garments were slashed, soaked and splattered with blood, and she saw all that too. As Lily stared at the male figure, she could no longer see the fierce expression; in its place was now a young visage, almost innocent looking, and she felt so much pity for him.

Lily sat beside him helplessly, trying to at least comfort him and relieve him of his pain.

Their eyes met as the man tried to speak, but his breath was coming slow and heavy.

"Friends are safe," he managed to mutter with some struggle, his expression gentle as he seized the front of her garments and pulled her in towards his face.

A terrible gurgling came from his throat as he tried to form words.

It seemed that he must have been drowning in his own blood and mucus.

"T … Take… Take it. Take my wand," he urged, stuttering as he gestured with his head at the wand in his palm. Lily looked down at it, then did as he said and carefully gripped it, feeling an immense warmth spreading through her; a green light enveloped her wrist and crept up the length of her arm, merging with her skin. She watched as his hand fell limply to the floor, blood seeping from the corner of his mouth. He weakly muttered in a strange language, and a swirling, silvery-blue light appeared a few feet away from them.

It was a portal, Lily realised.

"Go, please … go," he pleaded, nearly unable to form coherent words, his eyes wanting to close and say goodbye to this world. "Your friends, safe. Go …"

Lily would not go though, so she shook her head, not wanting to leave him there to die alone.

Their eyes locked, and he whispered something that made no sense to her.

"Olesia, do not be afraid."

Lily's mind raced. *These words don't make any sense,* she thought, but she would keep that to herself; now was not the time to question what he'd said. But who was Olesia, and why was he calling her by that name? Though admittedly, it was a pretty name.

In an instant, his eyes became lifeless, and he let out a final, heavy huff of exhalation.

The paper swallow that had been circling above dropped to the ground, its always fragile wings now become limp. Lily sobbed as she shook the dark wizard's lifeless body, desperate for him to wake again, but he remained unresponsive. His body was warm, and for a moment, she imagined he was still in the world of the living and would soon open his eyes.

It was just a way to make herself feel better. He had moved on, gone to the next plane.

But she would not just let him go in this way.

Desperately seeking a solution, Lily remembered the necklace that the old fortune teller lady had given her in the market. Hadn't the woman said it could bring back those who were near to death? Did she recall the woman's words correctly? She believed so.

So, she hastily removed the necklace, unscrewed the small lid on top of the vial, and tilted it over the man's lips, watching as the tiny droplets emerged one by one, slipping across his lips and trickling into his bloodied mouth. She could only hope that the elixir found its way to slip down his throat. Meanwhile, she cradled his head on her lap, waiting anxiously for any sign of life, but none came. She shook him again and again, but it was too late; he was already dead.

With tears streaming down her face, Lily whispered softly, "Thank you, whoever you were."

Never had she meant words more.

She clutched the wand tightly and stood up, wiping at her face and its salty tracks with the back of her hand. "So silly," she voiced to herself. "Crying like this over a complete stranger."

Lily heard the heavy sound of footsteps running up the hallway, the sound closing in on her; she needed to leave, right now. She looked up at the round, swirling silvery blue light that had now begun to close slowly. Even though she didn't want to leave Lord Cecil and Robert, she somehow knew they were safe and would eventually find her themselves.

She stood up, taking one last look at the man who had saved her, then walked over to the silvery-blue light. Lily jumped into it, bright bolts striking the ground beneath her.

The room began to spin, a tide of blinding darkness engulfing her as she felt pulled down into the abyss.

Argog, Lord Cecil, and Robert burst into the entrance of the grand hall. The scene awaiting them was one of utter devastation. Bodies littered the room, some still twitching from the electrical bolts, others lying motionless in pools of their own blood.

Carefully, the trio made their way farther into the hall, stumbling over the trail of bodies as they went, the crunch of bones underfoot making their stomachs churn. Lord Cecil covered his mouth with his hand, blocking out the stench of death pervading the air.

Argog ran over to the dark wizard, the man's motionless form lying there amidst all that carnage as if simply sleeping awhile. He collapsed to his knees, his wand clattering to the ground beside him as he let out a loud, harrowing wail of pain and anguish.

Lord Cecil and Robert felt the weight of his pain, the intensity of it, as if a physical force.

***

Lord Cecil gently held Robert by the arm, guiding him through the body piles, giving Argog a moment to himself. The two of them exchanged a worried glance, unsure of what to do in the face of such horror. What *could* they do? Apart from standing and staring, of course.

"Avert your eyes, boy. This is no sight for a child," Lord Cecil warned softly, but Robert didn't listen. He kept his eyes fixed on the bodies with a purpose, scanning through for Lily.

There was blood everywhere they stepped, some watery

and some beginning to clot in darkened congealing clumps. It stuck to the soles of their boots as if intent on taunting them, sticky and unwilling to let go, not allowing them to overlook the torture in this place.

The trail of bodies had been left as they'd fallen, broken and wide-eyed, with glassy stares.

The sight was gruesome and cold; their souls had left the bodies, the men now looking more like empty and distorted husks, beginning to grow blue and cold.

Robert shivered at the scene as humble tears tumbled down his cheeks, praying to the gods that Lily wasn't to be found among these carcasses. After surveying the bodies for another moment, he was certain. *Lily isn't here. She's not dead*, he thought.

The silvery-blue light was beginning to shrink farther into the distance; time was running out.

Argog pulled himself together as he rose to his feet and turned to Lord Cecil and Robert.

"There's no time! We must move!" he shouted, beckoning the two, who moved closer.

To Lord Cecil's and Robert's utter surprise, Argog picked them up in his arms yet again as if they were as light as a feather, throwing them into the swirling silvery-blue light.

Hesitantly, Argog gazed one last time at the dark wizard's body, then he turned, also leaping into the portal before it had a chance to vanish away.

***

A magnificent latticework of electrical energy crackled and hummed between the two stone pillars, casting a blinding bluish light that pulsed throughout the Great Hall of the abandoned city. The energy grew in intensity as a tall, wiry, red-caped figure of a man stepped gracefully out of the portal, his red cape sweeping through the dirt with each stride.

The imposing figure possessed an air of superiority and contagious confidence, evident in every stride. He surveyed the area around with sharp, piercing eyes, taking in the devastation.

As he stood at the entrance, he raised his wand and mouthed a few ancient words, swinging the wand in his palm. Old lanterns that hadn't been lit for many years instantly sprang into life, burning brightly with a reddish glow, illuminating the Great Hall in a yellow and red light.

The figure looked down at the hundreds of bodies and body parts strewn across the floor of the hall, his expression blank as he scanned the corpses.

The sounds of footsteps echoed around him as Mida, a goblin who was also Abaddon's most trusted advisor, surveyed the dead for any survivors with a handful of masked men.

Abaddon slowly walked between the bodies, observing with morbid curiosity.

"Over two hundred slain. Which army has done this deed?" Abaddon asked in a slow and lowered voice as he inched closer to Mida, towering over the small figure of the ugly goblin, dressed in a green robe.

"Not an army, my lord," Mida replied swiftly, his gaze fixed on the man on the ground. "A single wizard," he added briskly.

He swivelled his head, his gaze fixing on the man upon whom Mida had focused.

Mida raised his staff over the body of the dark wizard;

the long staff had a large and impressive emerald stone at its top, glowing with a greenish light from within, giving it a spectral transparent appearance. "Many forms of magic were exploited, some known, some forgotten, and some ancient," Mida said as he knelt and touched the lips of the dark wizard with one of his long, wrinkled fingers. He lifted his finger to his small nostrils, smelling the remnants of the potion before tasting it. "Old magic, enormously powerful; it must be the Norn's doing,"

Abaddon stopped in his tracks. "The Weird Sisters," he grumbled to himself, unimpressed.

Mida stood and looked up at the tall figure of Abaddon, towering over his own small figure. "His wounds should have killed him, but their potion healed him of his mortal wounds."

***

"He lives?" Abaddon muttered, his eyes lingering on the dark wizard's still form.

"My lord. It is imperative that we study him and learn what he knows," Mida suggested, his voice betraying a hint of curiosity and greed.

Abaddon gave a long and considered pause. "Very well," he agreed, his voice carrying an undercurrent of intrigue. Strong curiosity gripped him.

He wanted to understand who this man was and why he was protecting the girl. He looked around the Great Hall once again, taking in the dead dispersed across the floor. Then, Abaddon's attention was suddenly drawn to a rustling sound emanating from the cold, hard stone floor.

He peered down to see a small paper bird twitching as if struggling to take flight. As if panicked, the bird flapped its wings and soared into the air, frantically circling the Great Hall as if searching for someone before homing and swooping down towards Abaddon in a suicide dive.

Without batting an eyelid, Abaddon calmly waved his wand, causing the bird to freeze in mid-air, just inches from his face. As if intrigued by the sight before him, Abaddon examined the bird, twirling and spinning it, gently prodding it with his wand.

Unsure of what to make of such sorcery, Abaddon looked on curiously, taking in every detail of the paper bird. "What form of enchantment is this?" Abaddon queried, captivated by the simplicity and power of such wizardry.

"I do not know, my lord," Mida said cautiously, as if not wishing to upset Abaddon.

Nonetheless, Abaddon was astonished by Mida's answer. Didn't he know everything there was to know about magic? Abaddon, out of annoyance, abruptly flicked his wand, and a bright flame erupted from the tip of the paper bird, engulfing it in a fierce and fiery inferno.

As the paper bird slowly disintegrated, burning bits of black paper floated away into the air of the Great Hall. As the last remnants of the bird burned away, Abaddon noticed how the black ash floated like smoke, twirling and dancing on the currents of air.

After a few moments. Abaddon stormed off with purpose to the entrance, waving his wand in the air as he moved. The bluish light flashed between the two stone pillars.

Abaddon stepped into the flashing light and disappeared along with it.

Chapter Nine:
The Pursuit of Fate

Radiant beams of sunlight pierced through the murky clouds, painting the horizon with shades of gold and orange. As the shadows of the clouds descended upon the tranquil waters below, the wind sang a haunting melody in the distance, accompanied by the roar of the waves as they crashed against the caves and rocks.

The sound echoed all around, engulfing the air with its power.

Above the earth, a striking seagull with a white-grey head soared through a deep, dark sky, surveying the land with hungry eyes. Its gaze settled on someone. Perched atop a rugged and jagged cliff, there stood a strange and withered old woman, her gaze fixed on the expansive open fields in the distance. She wore a long, black cloak that had faded with time, and her grey, lengthy hair was knotted behind her head, swaying with the salty wind.

In the distance, the slender wild grass shimmered in the stiff coastal breeze.

Without warning, a blinding blue light burst forth, growing wider and more vivid.

Lily emerged from the portal, her appearance slightly disoriented as a strong gust of cold, salty wind threw dirt in her face. Recoiling to protect herself, she shuddered as the wind howled through the fields, causing her thin clothes to flap against her skin, making her teeth clatter.

All alone in this unfamiliar place, her mind immediately went to Robert and Lord Cecil.

Were they safe? Her thoughts then drifted to the horrific carnage witnessed earlier, and to the man who had saved her despite being a stranger. Why had he done it?

As the fierce wind blew even stronger, Lily grew colder, her body jittering uncontrollably.

Standing there, alone and afraid, Lily's thoughts were interrupted by a sudden feeling of warmth and a gentle blue light emanating from her wand.

Exhaling softly, Lily faced the wind and accepted her fate.

She began to run through the vast expanse of open fields. The wind whipped her hair around her face as she ran, causing it to whip back and forth like the wild grasses around.

A prickling sensation spread across her skin, accompanied by the unmistakable sense of being watched. Panic began to set in, sensing danger lurking nearby.

She tightened her grip on her wand and darted forward, her legs pumping as fast as they could, each stride propelling her closer to safety.

Yet, the feeling of being pursued lingered, and she couldn't shake the image of a pack of savage wolves nipping at her heels. With each passing moment, the urgency of her flight intensified, and she strained against the limits of her physical endurance. The distant unknown horizon seemed to stretch out endlessly before her, a vast and open expanse.

Perched high atop the craggy overhang, the haggard old lady cast a watchful gaze.

Muttering to herself in a foreign language, she spoke in a trance-like state, her words a cryptic and ancient incantation. The winds, attuned to the old hag's will, whipped around her, carrying her voice far and wide. She fell silent, as if her attention had been drawn to the young girl running through the fields below.

With a sly grin, the old hag spoke again, her words carrying the weight of prophecy.

"Behold, dear child, your destiny beckons," she whispered.

Her laughter boomed like thunder, a tempestuous symphony echoing through valleys and hills.

Chapter Ten:
Tremors of the Past

Abaddon made his way through the maze-like network of narrow and dark underground passageways. It was a dark and dreary place, the silence only disturbed by the soft dripping of water seeping through the small stalactites from above, and the occasional harrowing screams and shrieks of pain. The air was thick with muddy dampness, making it difficult to breathe.

The darkness was so relentless that it was impossible to see more than a few feet ahead. The only other light in the passageway came from the tip of Abaddon's wand, but it was no match for the darkness that encompassed and subdued its very essence, sucking it in.

Deep within the labyrinthine bowels of the cave, an ancient crone resided in a desolate chamber shrouded in darkness, illuminated only by the faint glow of phosphorescent fungi growing along its walls. The air was thick with the stench of mould and decay.

The crone herself was a grotesque figure, with a hunched and twisted body adorned in tattered rags accompanied by writhing, matted hair. From behind the metal limits of her cell, her sunken eyes glowed with a malevolent light, fixed intently upon a small, shallow pool of water at the centre of the chamber. With a sudden lunge, she snatched up a hapless rodent that scurried across the stone floor, sinking jagged teeth into its flesh without a moment's hesitation.

The rat writhed in agony, squealing in pain before falling limp in the crone's grasp.

As the lifeblood of the creature trickled into the pool at her feet, the water churned and frothed. A strange, otherworldly energy filled the air, and an image formed within the depths of the pool. Lily appeared, running through a field of long and wild grass.

The crone's calculating gaze remained fixed upon the vision before her, her sunken eyes gleaming with intensity. Her thin lips curled into a sly smirk and, with a rasping, guttural voice, she murmured, "I see sister." But the moment was abruptly shattered by the heavy tread of boots from down the passageway. The sound grew louder and closer. The crone swivelled her head towards the source of the noise, her calculating gaze replaced with a sly grin as she purred under her breath, "By the pricking of my thumb, something wicked this way comes."

As if in response, she dipped a bony finger into the pool and stirred the image, causing it to dissolve into shimmering ripples. The water slowly returned to a placid state, concealing the vision of the young girl running through the fields.

Abaddon approached, rattling the cell bars with a furious glare. The crone remained undaunted, her twisted lips curling into a wry smile as she regarded her captor.

"What have you done, you devious old hag?" Abaddon snarled.

The crone let out a soft cackle, revealing a mouthful of decaying teeth and a face mapped by deep creases that seemed to swallow up her eyes.

Abaddon demanded, "Show me who he is."

The crone grinned with delight.

"The wisdom I possess will show the sands of time and seeds so small, will bring to light the echoes of past, the memories that call," replied the witch. She then grabbed a small wooden goblet from a low-lying bench at the back of her cell and seized a wooden spoon to scoop some murky liquid from a small boiling pot into the goblet.

The witch slid the wooden goblet through the sturdy iron bars of the cell, handing it to Abaddon. He approached it cautiously, giving the contents a careful sniff before quickly downing the elixir. The magic potion took an immediate grip on him, causing him to drop the goblet onto the cold stone floor with a loud clatter. As the potion coursed through his veins, he turned and leaned against the bars, violently convulsing and jerking as his body reacted to the powerful magic. Once he settled, he sat down and began to randomly fire his wand at some invisible foe in the air. A lightning bolt shot out and collided with the rocky wall, causing debris to fly and a cloud of dust to fill the musty dungeon.

With a gradual easing, a peaceful sensation enveloped him, like a gentle wave lapping at the shores of his consciousness. Suddenly, an image appeared with crystal clarity.

A man peered down at the dark wizard, now turned into a quivering adolescent boy. Abaddon instantly recognised the man standing over the boy as Selwyn, a wizard he had slain years ago.

"No matter what you hear or witness, keep yourself concealed until I return," Selwyn instructed the boy, before closing the door of the rickety outhouse behind him.

The man sprinted toward a village that was engulfed in flames. Abaddon peered through one of the cracks in the outhouse, seeing a younger version of himself appearing nearby.

Turning swiftly, Selwyn unleashed a volley of brilliant blue lightning bolts from his wand at the shadowy figure looming behind. The younger, masked Abaddon—though momentarily taken aback by the sudden onslaught—deftly deflected the incoming bolts with his wand.

The two circled each other in the dimly lit surroundings.

Selwyn attempted to draw Abaddon away from the outhouse by edging backward. As he retreated, he reached into his inner garments, pulling out a handful of bang poppers and hurling them at Abaddon in a desperate attempt to divert his attention.

However, Abaddon, with a swift flick of his wand, effortlessly dispelled the ploy.

Undeterred, Selwyn reached into one of his outer pockets and retrieved a pouch of ebony powder. With a swift gesture, he now hurled this at Abaddon, engulfing him in an inky shroud of darkness. But Abaddon was quick to adapt, spinning to pinpoint Selwyn's position.

Abaddon brandished his wand with lightning speed, unleashing a barrage of short, crackling bursts of lightning bolts towards Selwyn.

Selwyn desperately attempted to deflect Abaddon's relentless strikes, but he proved too slow, and the flurry of bolts overcame him. He tumbled to the ground, disoriented and defeated.

The boy watched as if in horror, tears welling as Abaddon observed the trembling figure before him. Abaddon felt a palpable vulnerability not known since childhood.

The scene disintegrated, reshaping into a new portrayal, a canvas in constant flux.

***

Gently swaying in the soft dusk breeze, tall river reeds resembled a graceful dance. In the distance, the sounds of battle cries, explosions and thick black smoke billowed on the far horizon. Beyond the lily reeds was an open clearing, where a giant Herne crouched on his knees, carefully and dexterously picking wild mushrooms from the ground with his large fur hands.

The Herne's heightened senses detectd the unmistakable sound of a transportation device zooming through the air. His acute senses also enabled him to perceive the palpable aura of blood and terror emanating from a young boy and a small girl, both of whom were attempting to conceal themselves amidst the river reeds just beyond the entrance of the field. He recognised that they were of no harm to him, and he continued to gather the mushrooms with a watchful eye.

Abruptly, the Herne's acute senses detected approaching footsteps in the marshy wetland.

As he listened intently, he deduced that they belonged to a group of five humans, moving with both haste and purpose. The Herne's eyes narrowed.

As the five masked figures came into the clearing, they recoiled in terror and their eyes fixated on the imposing figure before them.

They cautiously inched their way forward, wary of the Herne's massive frame.

The Herne was only kneeling, yet still he towered over them, casting a long shadow that stretched across the ground, foreshadowing the danger ahead.

With slow and deliberate steps, they advanced, wary of the Herne's massive frame. The figures formed a loose circle around him.

"Watch your step. He could take us down with a single blow," warned one of the figures.

Another called out to the rest of the group, "Where's his wand?"

The Herne remained unperturbed by their presence, continuing to gather his mushrooms with quiet determination. His attention never wavered from his task, as if the figures in masks were nothing more than mere distractions.

One of the figures behind him shouted, "Kill him!"

Yet, their attention was quickly diverted by a single firework bursting into the sky with only a soft bang, causing them to look up. Just then, a rustling came from the river reeds, and one of the masked figures fired his wand indiscriminately in the direction of the sound.

The other masked figures followed suit, unleashing a barrage of electric bolts from their wands in a flurry of panicked energy. However, in what seemed like mere seconds, the Herne had swiftly incapacitated all five of the masked figures with his bare hands.

Their broken and bloody bodies lay strewn across the grassy area as if fallen out of the sky.

Rushing towards the river reeds, the Herne found a young boy lying helplessly on the ground in a pool of blood, with a multitude of shallow wounds across his chest.

The boy lay weeping and in too much pain to move, while a small toddler girl who had been hiding with him gazed up at the towering Herne, petrified.

With gentle care, the Herne knelt down beside the wounded boy, pulling out his wand and muttering a soothing spell in a foreign tongue.

Waving his wand over the boy's injuries, the Herne managed to heal the wounds instantly, relief immediately apparent on the boy's face.

"The name I bear is Argog," said the Herne with a softness that contradicted his immense and intimidating presence.

The image swirled and swished around, then slowly came into focus, fleeting yet vivid.

The teenage boy stood silently beside Argog as he gently handed over the toddler girl to an older couple who appeared grateful.

Another image began to sharpen, a new scene emerging, and the teenage boy had transformed into a young man. Now, he was clad entirely in black garments, with his cape fluttering vigorously in the gusty wind as Argog stood beside him. Standing resolute, the young man gazed fixedly at a small opening on the opposite cliff face that the Herne had pointed out.

Argog's voice was almost inaudible amidst the deafening cacophony of the storm as he shouted, "There!" The two were standing on a precarious craggy ledge, jutting from the cliffs. The atmosphere was dense with tension. Grey clouds hung low, pregnant with menace, and the wind raged, lashing the landscape with its wild abandon. The rain was an unrelenting deluge, heavy drops swirling and twisting amidst the howling gusts.

Together, they manoeuvred through hazardous and narrow maze paths that led them deeper into caves, with the tips of their wands the only source of light, the damp musty air clinging to their skin. Finally, they arrived at an opening that led to a large, dark cave chamber.

Argog ran his hands over the surrounding rocks.

"Goblin magic," he murmured. "The enchantments are too strong for me to override. Only one can enter." The young man strode forward with confidence, but Argog quickly intervened, blocking his path with his large muscular arm.

"Beware," Argog cautioned. "Goblin magic is not to be trifled with. It will test you. It will exploit your deepest fears."

The young man stepped into the cavernous opening, his wand at the ready as he moved forward with caution. He flicked his wand, creating a beam of light that illuminated the cavern's dark interior, casting eerie shadows on the walls.

As he ventured farther into the depths of the cave, his attention was drawn to a stirring on the ground before him. As he muttered an incantation, a dazzling orb shot out of his wand and soared high above, momentarily illuminating the entire cavern in a bright glow.

The floor seethed with a tangled mass of serpents, a living nightmare come true, and the young man's terror surged, for there was nothing in the world he feared more.

But undeterred, he cast another spell, and the snakes parted to form a narrow path on which he could tread. Moving with the utmost care, he kept a close watch on the writhing reptiles.

One of the snakes hissed, slithering towards him.

In a flash, he swung his wand and unleashed a bolt of lightning, striking the snake with deadly force, sending it hurtling across the cave floor.

At the cavern's core, nestled amidst the dark shadows, stood a stone dais flanked by three rough-hewn steps, leading to a low-lying platform.

The young man carefully clambered up the steps, his eyes fixed on the old tome that lay upon a stone mantle. Its leather cover was weathered and worn by the ravages of time, yet it still emanated a mysterious aura, drawing him closer.

As he approached the mantle, he scanned the area for any sign of magical enchantments or curses. He picked up a small rock and hurled it towards the book, only to watch it vanish upon collision with a surrounding invisible force field.

The young man tried spell after spell, pacing back and forth.

The hours crept by as he battled to breach the book's impregnable defences, but to no avail. Despite his best efforts, the young man remained locked in a seemingly endless stalemate with the enchantment before him, the silence of the cavern echoing with his frustration.

The young man sat down in utter exhaustion and frustration, his eyes falling upon a venomous snake that had made its way onto the platform. With an angry flick of his wand, a surge of lightning was released, hitting the serpent with lethal power and launching it across the cavern's rocky surface. Then, he whispered under his breath, "I wonder …"

Taking a deep breath, he muttered a spell, and his wand sparked and glowed, emitting a powerful yellow light that took the shape of a giant snake.

With a swift and precise motion, he yanked his wand back as if pulling a rope around the snake made of light, then forcefully pointed it at the stone mantle, commanding it to attack.

The stone mantle shuddered and cracked as the snake of light slithered and coiled around it, chipping away at the book's defences.

The young man watched the snake continue its relentless assault until, with a final energy burst, the force field shattered, the book lying unprotected before him.

The young man carefully hoisted the tome and gingerly deposited it into a satchel concealed deftly beneath his cloak. His euphoria at having successfully dispelled the powerful enchantment was brief, as he caught sight of a nest of writhing serpents undulating towards him on the platform. In a frenzied attempt to ward off the venomous creatures, he waved his wand frantically, only to end up aghast. The wand had snapped in two, rendering it entirely ineffectual.

It was a cruel and calculated parting gift from the potent enchantment, designed to hinder any potential raider's chances of escaping the perilous cavern alive.

The young man sprinted through the ever-narrowing path he had created amid the sea of serpents. His pace quickened as the space around him grew ever more constricted, and he just managed to reach the entrance to the cave, where Argog was patiently waiting.

A mere moment's delay would almost certainly have resulted in his death.

He looked back at the trail he had just blazed and noticed that the cave floor was now entirely barren, devoid of any trace of the deadly snakes that had threatened his life moments before.

"Why would he go to such lengths to protect an old, ragged book?" asked the young man.

"Perhaps it holds a link to his past. Something he wishes

to hide," replied Argog, carefully examining the tome.

"Why not simply destroy it then?" The young man furrowed his brow in deep thought as he continued searching for answers. "The prophecy clearly states that no man alive can defeat him. Perhaps it contains some clue about Abaddon's weakness?'"

"I do not know," informed Argog. He fixed his gaze on the old tome before him. "The writing is encoded. We'll require the exact goblin spell to decipher it."

"You'll need another wand," said Argog, tucking the tome into a spacious pocket nestled within his inner garment. With his other hand, he retrieved a folded felt cloth and unfurled it, revealing three wands inside. The young man surveyed them all briefly before selecting the slightly shorter, dark brown wand situated at the right edge.

"Wild oak, a sturdy and reliable choice," confirmed Argog with a nod.

***

Abaddon's mind became a turbulent sea, churning with a whirlwind of thoughts and emotions as the elixir continued to work on his mind and body. With each passing moment, it seemed to conjure up a new image. And yet, amidst the chaos, there was a glimmer of something else, perhaps his own memory that Abaddon had tried so hard to forget.

As he fought to push the image away, he could feel the weight of it pressing down upon him, threatening to engulf him entirely.

A small, thatched cottage adorned with a wild garden, nestled under the grey, cloudy sky.

It sat alone in the midst of an expansive landscape of untamed grass and open fields, where small rocky hills and craggy overhangs dotted the terrain here and there.

The wind, intermittent and chillingly salty, whipped and lashed the wild grasses, causing them to bend and sway in its force. Amidst the sounds of waves crashing against the cliff and the occasional cry of gulls, a gentle stream of smoke wafted out of the cottage's chimney.

The wooden door of the cottage creaked open, and a small room revealed itself within, where a fire blazed merrily in the fireplace. Adjacent to the fireplace stood a metal stove, where a large black pot of soup bubbled and brewed over the flames, filling the air with an inviting aroma.

Inside the room was a blind old man with ghostly, milky-white eyes that seemed to stare off into the abyss. His face was lined with deep wrinkles, telling a story of a long and hard life.

Strands of silver hair were scattered haphazardly around his head, giving the appearance of a weathered and ancient tree. His clothing, long and tattered, hung loosely on his frail frame.

He leaned heavily on a wooden cane, each step slow and measured as if every movement was an act of defiance against the inevitability of age.

The old man hobbled over to the fire, his cane tapping on the stone floor with each step, like a gentle melody accompanying his movements. He prodded the embers with the end of his cane, coaxing the flames to grow brighter and stronger.

With an iron fire shovel, he scooped some of the ash from the fireplace and placed it into a wooden bucket, careful not to spill any on the floor. As he made his way outside, the wind tugged at his clothing and sent strands of his silver hair flying in all directions. It was as if he were a wise sage tending to the needs of nature, embracing his barren surroundings.

As he shuffled about in his garden, gingerly digging the wild and coarse soil with his cane and mixing in some of the ash with the earth, the old man seemed to feel the presence of someone who stood silently watching him, like a shadow lurking in the corner. He looked up briefly.

Then he continued with his earth works as if he had sensed and seen nothing at all.

The old man's gnarled fingers dug down into the soil, unearthing a few stubborn rocks and roots as he worked, his face crinkling in concentration, unaffected by the peculiar presence.

Abaddon twisted and contorted his body in frustration, as if he could physically shake off the memory. His muscles tensed, and his jaw clenched tight as he tried to push the image away.

But the memory persisted.

"This soil will never yield anything of worth," a voice dripped with a mocking tone.

Abaddon watched from his mind's eye as his younger self interacted with the old man, the words and actions feeling foreign and distant.

The old man chuckled wryly, his voice carrying the wisdom of ages. "Ah, but you see, it is precisely because this soil is barren that I will be able to grow unique and hardy plants. They thrive on adversity, and the ash from my fire will nourish them. Astonishing that something as destructive as fire can birth something as beautiful and poetic as life itself."

Abaddon's eyebrow rose in surprise as he listened intently to the old man's wise words.

With great effort, the old man rose from his knees, leaning heavily on his gnarled wooden cane, and stretched out a trembling hand to touch Abaddon's face. But as his fingers drew near, the old man hesitated, as though sensing a danger that Abaddon himself could not perceive.

The old man chuckled, then said, "Sight may capture the world's façade, but truth lies beyond what eyes applaud—"

Abaddon cut in, finishing his phrase for him. "In darkness, I find wisdom's grace, revealing beauty beyond a physical trace."

"You remember. If only you had learnt its morals," the old man softly said with a hint of regret.

Abaddon's mind screamed in protest, violent and tumultuous as he tried to break free from the memory's hold. He could feel the weight of it bearing down on him, suffocating and overwhelming. With a fierce determination, Abaddon pushed back against it, willing himself to forget. And slowly but surely, he felt the memory begin to fade until it was nothing more than a faint echo in the back of his mind.

As another image began to solidify once more, Abaddon found himself looking upon a young couple, lying together on a blanket spread across a lush green field.

He was certain this was the same young wizard. There was a beautiful young lady lying beside him, long black hair cascading down her olive skin, framing big, mesmerising brown eyes. They shone with a warmth and kindness that seemed to envelop Abaddon in their embrace.

The young man looked content beside the woman, as if

the world around him didn't matter.

They gazed up at the endless expanse of the clear blue sky, lost in their own little world of love and happiness. Argog sat at a respectful distance, as if observing the natural sounds around him, and as though he was careful not to disturb the young couple's serene moment.

The young lady turned her head towards the young man and posed a question, her inquisitive eyes gleaming in the afternoon sun. "Why does Argog trail behind you so?"

The young man let out a soft laugh, his eyes sparkling with amusement. For a moment, he remained silent, as if contemplating his response.

"It's unheard of for a Herne to be in the company of a human," she continued, her curiosity getting the better of her.

The young man turned towards her, revealing a gentle smile.

"You need not be afraid of him," he said, his voice reassuring.

The girl's lips curved upwards, her expression radiating warmth. "Oh, you misunderstand. I am not afraid. I was merely curious," she responded.

After a brief moment of reflection, the young man spoke again. "You know, they say love is one of the most powerful forms of magic. Have you ever heard people say that?"

A soft breeze blew past them, rustling the leaves of the nearby trees.

The girl's eyes softened, and she extended her hand towards him, her fingers tracing the contours of his face. "There is something I need to tell you," she whispered, a hint of nervousness evident in her voice. "I am with child."

At first, the young man seemed taken aback, his

expression one of surprise. He moved away swiftly a foot or so, resting back on his hands, staring wide-eyed at her.

But he quickly recovered, enfolding her in a warm and close embrace.

Another image gradually sharpened into focus, gusts of wind relentlessly battering a dark and dreary terrain, arcs of lightning illuminating the atmosphere. A solitary stone edifice loomed over the desolate moor. Upon entering, he beheld midwives adorned with rectangular headgear and pristine white robes, scurrying along a dimly lit corridor illuminated by wildly flickering candles mounted on the walls. The anxious young man paced back and forth within the cramped confines of the space, striving to attract the attention of the busy midwives.

They remained indifferent, darting past, pretending not to even notice his presence.

An older gentleman—unmistakably a physician draped in a lengthy white medical gown strolled along the lengthy, dark, stone corridor, trailed by a coterie of midwives. The clack of their footsteps reverberated loudly through the cold stone hallway.

The physician approached the agitated young man, who had been pacing back and forth in a frenzied state. "I am afraid I have some distressing news," he said tentatively.

The young man appeared bewildered, his anxiety palpable.

"The child?" he inquired nervously.

The physician paused for a moment, as if attempting to determine the most suitable approach. "I am sorry to inform you that they did not survive."

The room appeared to spin out of control, and the young man, disoriented, responded, "They? Who are you referring to? I demand to speak with my wife." He went pallid, his legs giving way.

"She has passed away," the physician responded. "Both she and the child are no more."

The young man violently shoved the physician against the rough-hewn wall, knocking the wind out of him. He brandished his wand, pressing the tip against the physician's throat.

"You are lying, you wretched slave!" he exclaimed. "Don't stand there, telling me they died!"

The physician, likely nervous for his life, implored the young man, "We did everything within our power. Everything! I cannot even tell you how hard we—"

The image faded, twisted, swirled.

The next image came into focus, revealing a moonless night.

The young man materialised with a tattered and haggard appearance, his clothes in disarray and his face gaunt with exhaustion. With manic frenetic gestures, he brandished his wand, unleashing furious lightning bolts that crackled through the air. The bolts struck Abaddon's masked followers, causing them to fall in bloody heaps, lifeless.

The young man stood amidst the carnage, his eyes blazing with fierce determination.

The bodies of Abaddon's minions lay strewn across the ground, their once imposing masks shattered and broken. Standing by himself, the young man bore a deep and lengthy bloody cut on his left cheek. His wand remained raised high, its tip fizzing with energy.

A woman leading a group of children navigated through the gruesome field, urging the young ones to avert their eyes from the carnage.

The children, clutching each other's hands, did as they were told and trod behind the woman in single file, scaling a low stone wall to reach the other side. The young man, watching their progress with cold detachment, ignored the woman's grateful words, turning instead towards Argog standing farther up the hill, gripping a helpless goblin by the collar.

Argog gazed at the dark wizard, his expression emotionless. "He doesn't know the spell to unlock the tome. Hapless one …"

"Then what use is he?" the dark wizard queried, raising his wand to strike the goblin dead.

"Wait! I will give you information even more valuable!" pleaded the goblin, who had a squashed-looking face, wrinkled skin, and a tiny snub nose.

The young man, now a powerful dark wizard, grinned wickedly. "And pray tell me what that might be?" He lowered his wand, his voice dripping with malice.

"The most powerful wand ever created," the goblin whispered in hushed tones.

The dark wizard scoffed back, "Indeed, so you say. I have heard them a thousand times, such far-fetched stories, and they always end the same way."

The goblin's eyes widened in panic, and he struggled to speak.

"But it is true. I know precisely where it lies. All you have to do is spare my life." He paused, his chest heaving as he fought for breath. "It belonged to the great White Witch of the North. And I do know where it resides. If you wish to have any chance of killing Abaddon, then you'll need it.

That's what you want, isn't it? To kill Abaddon." His eyes darted nervously around.

The dark wizard raised his wand, ready to strike the goblin down. The image flickered before Abaddon's eyes, revealing a picturesque scene of a young boy and girl playing amongst some abandoned ruins, hidden among the dense foliage of the surrounding trees.

Argog and the dark wizard stood in the shadows, silently observing the innocent scene, the boy and girl remaining blissfully unaware of their presence.

As the image faded, unease settled in Abaddon's chest. He knew that this was the girl from the Norn's prophecy. Abaddon raised his wand and sent a bolt of lightning hurtling toward her, trying to strike and kill the girl in the image. However, the bolt instead struck the rocky wall opposite where Abaddon sat, sending shards of stone flying in every direction. Debris filled the air. As the dust began to settle, Abaddon's frustration grew as the image started to fade.

The next image presented a rugged mountain range, its peaks veiled by dense clouds. The dark wizard and Argog were scaling a treacherous mountain face, battling fierce gusts of snow and wind that buffeted their bodies. After what seemed like an eternity, they finally reached the summit and continued along the narrow ridge until they came upon a massive boulder.

Without hesitation, Argog fired a bolt of magic into the ground, causing the frozen earth and snow to erupt in a blinding shower of white.

The dust settling, a shallow grave came into view, and within it lay the perfectly preserved corpse of a woman, her skin and features seemingly untouched by time. She was draped in a white cloak and garment, her long white hair cascading over her shoulders.

In her right hand, she held a long, pointed wand, its delicate patterns gleaming in the icy light.

The dark wizard hesitated a moment, eyeing the corpse warily. But with a nod of encouragement from Argog, he reached for the wand grasped in the woman's hand.

Carefully prying it loose, he held it aloft, studying its intricate carvings.

And as he did, a green light enveloped his wrist, creeping up his arm until it merged with his skin. He tested its power by pointing it towards the sky, and with a crackling burst of energy, a bright lightning bolt shot forth, illuminating the snowy landscape.

Abaddon was abruptly jolted from his trance by the searing brightness of the wand's lightning. The intensity of the flash shook him from his deep meditative state, leaving him gasping for air and struggling to regain his bearings amidst the sudden disorientation that followed.

"Show me more," he implored the witch, his voice thick with desperation. His tone was raw and urgent, his eyes locking onto hers as he begged her to reveal his past.

"Unveil, unveil, unveil his eyes and burden his heart," she breathed into his ear, her voice barely audible as he submitted to the dark magic of the witch. "Enter like shadows, fading away."

And with those words, he was flung through a pitch-black void at a dizzying speed, hurtling deeper into the abyss. The darkness enveloped him like a suffocating blanket, propelling him through time and space, the memories of the dark wizard's past swirling around him in a kaleidoscope of emotions and sensations.

The darkness surrounding Abaddon pulsed with malevolent energy. After the brief distortion, an image gradually settled and came into focus once more, revealing a scene of eeriness.

A dismal grey clenched the air, and far off, a storm of floating clouds drifted as lightning flashed across the sky in an elaborate splinter over a grim horizon.

A man shivered under the frigid wind blowing over the spindly and barren land, his jacket billowing in the breeze as he wrapped his arms around himself. A thick mist engulfed the cold and gloomy landscape, leaving it, to the naked eye, mysterious and infinite. There was silence, disturbed only by the whistling of the wind bitterly blowing across the marshy ground.

He stood all by himself under a large monolithic tree. From one of the low, thick branches, an old witch was hanging from a rope; her neck was broken, her head canted to one side with her dirty grey hair loitering on her pale green face. Her visage was contorted and scarred, and even though the witch was dead, her glassy brown eyes still managed to give an accusing stare.

The rope made a creaking noise as the dead body swayed , blown by the cold strong wind. The odious stench of the hanging corpse haunted the vicinity, maggots writhing in deep holes within the abdomen and chest, freeing yellowed, dripping, sticky pus to the earth.

It was a horrifying sight, one that would leave any man's dreams haunted. Beyond the tree lay a small, dilapidated cottage that stood empty. Abaddon looked on in fascination.

He pulled out his wand and his dark magic osculator detector. A small and weighty apparatus, was crafted from black iron and set with a central, smoky crystal. Fine copper filigree wrapped around its edges. He cautiously approaching the cottage. The wooden door had been forced off its hinges, and he slowly stepped over the threshold and entered. The interior of the small cottage was dark and shadowed; the only light dimly illuminating the room came from a small broken window at the wall's far end.

The room stank of dead and rotten things, and he covered his nose as he walked through the pile of dirt, his eyes darting around the room for any sign of dark items.

Various-sized bottles and jars filled with curious-looking roots, herbs, plants, and other objects stood on shelves lining the walls. He waved his wand in a quick clockwise motion, and the end of his wand lit up orange. The glow from the wand's tip gave a modest circle of light to the encroaching darkness. His osculator hummed with excitement as he made his way around a large oak table in the middle of the room and towards a staircase.

Still, he proceeded, and as he did, the osculator began to vibrate and hum with greater excitement, directing him to an area in the room's corner. He raised his wand higher, ready for whatever it was as he moved forward. He was full of anticipation as he approached the dark corner; here, the wand's light revealed a terrified young boy wrapped in a blanket, crouching in the darkness. He instantly lowered his wand, not to frighten the youngster. Abaddon continued to watch in his inner thoughts, promptly discerning the boy as the dark wizard.

The osculator hummed out of control, and the man

looked on in total confusion; he had never experienced this before, but seeing the fear in the boy's eyes, he crouched before him, tucking the wand inside his harness as he stretched out his right hand to him.

"Do not be afraid," he said softly, flashing the boy a sweet smile. "My name is Selwyn. What's yours?" The boy didn't answer. "I won't hurt you, I promise."

Selwyn waited, gesturing to the boy to take his hand.

The boy hesitantly held out his own hand, placing it over Selwyn's.

Selwyn gripped the lad's hand firmly, he and the boy making their way across the desolate and barren land. The boy hadn't spoken a single word the entire time they'd walked, and Selwyn finally stopped to look around as he pulled a small wooden flute-like instrumentfrom his brown overcoat.

He held it out to the boy.

"Here, touch it with your hands, and don't let go," Selwyn commanded as he knelt in front of the boy. However, his attention was quickly drawn to the fluttering above his head.

As he looked up to the grey sky, a paper bird in the shape of a swallow hovered, circled, and called out high and sweet. Selwyn looked down at the boy and smiled at him momentarily, before peering up again to marvel at the beauty of the paper bird.

Chapter Twelve:
Gadabout The Great

As dusk draped its velvet shroud upon the countryside, a wizard bedecked in a pointy blue hat and a long blue robe adorned with yellow stars strolled cheerfully along an uneven, narrow lane bordered by green meadows and sporadic small woodlands.

Trailing behind him, a disheartened young man was moving with little enthusiasm.

Two unsavoury figures emerged unexpectedly from the shadows behind a hedge bordering the lane. The first, towering and skeletal, exhibited a face swollen with malevolence, while the second, compact and robust, showcased an oddly large and distorted nose.

The taller man pointed his wand with menace at the wizard, while the shorter raised his wand toward the young companion.

"How can I be of assistance to you fine gentlemen on this beautiful evening?" inquired the colourful wizard, his words delicate and meditative as if trying to weave a spell to soothe the tension surrounding this unexpected encounter.

"Who are you?" demanded the taller man.

"I am Gadabout the Great, and this is my trusty assistant, Randolph. I am a world-famous performer. Perhaps you've seen one of my stage shows?"

The two men gave no reaction. "We're under orders to locate some persons of interest," the taller man barked, a subtle intensity in his gaze conveying the urgency of their mission.

"Well, we don't really pique anyone's interest, unless, of course, it's under the spotlight. Maybe you've caught wind—" Gadabout paused momentarily, catching a whiff of an unpleasant smell emanating from the shorter man. He coughed and continued, "Perhaps you've heard the rave reviews of my numerous enchanting magical spectacles and marvels. How about a demonstration right now?"

Gadabout seemed eager to find a quick and clever escape from their current predicament.

"Search him," the taller man commanded. The other complied with alacrity, aggressively patting down Gadabout while inspecting the myriad pockets of his long, vibrant jacket.

He pulled out Gadabout's wand and tossed it to the ground.

The taller man turned his attention to Randolph.

"Where's your wand, boy?" he barked as he forcefully ripped open the young man's lengthy brown jacket, conducting a thorough pat down of his inner shirt.

"I don't have one, sir."

"Why not?" quizzed the taller man with suspicion.

"I've given up violence, sir. And wands are tools of mass destruction that perpetuate the violent side of magic, sir. Wizards don't kill people, sir. Wands do."

"Is there something wrong with him?" asked the taller man.

"Yes, he's a complete simpleton," Gadabout responded. "That's what's wrong with him."

The short man continued his search of Gadabout, unearthing an assortment of peculiar objects that should have been too big to fit inside his jacket.

From Gadabout's left pocket, he pulled out an unending procession of colourful handkerchiefs, all inexplicably knotted together, leaving the two men bewildered.

"Enough of this nonsense," asserted the taller man, shoving his companion aside. He forcefully ripped open Gadabout's jacket, delving into his pockets to retrieve a meticulously folded pencil drawing of a striking younger man.

He directed his sharp gaze at Gadabout. "Who's this?" he demanded.

"Ah, no one special. Just an old dear friend I once knew," Gadabout replied with a smile, though his eyes betrayed a different tale as he struggled to maintain his composure.

The tall man grinned, revealing yellow and black-stained teeth.

"A friend, you say?" His eyes narrowed as he scrutinised Gadabout, then he aggressively seized Gadabout's left arm and rolled up his lengthy sleeve, revealing a substantial circular black tattoo. The man forcefully jabbed his wand so hard against the skin of the tattoo that blood trickled from the pressure. "You were once a convict?"

Gadabout continued to smile.

"Is it a crime to love?" he gently inquired, peering at the tall man pleadingly.

The shorter man, who had been searching Randolph, shouted, "Look at this," holding up a piece of parchment featuring a black ink drawing of a swallow.

"What's this?" inquired the taller man, eyeing the ink drawing.

"A drawing of a swallow, sir," Randolph replied with an impassive deadpan expression and a monotone voice. "The swallow … it's a bird, sir."

"I know what it is. But what does it mean?" He sounded most annoyed.

"It's a symbol of re-res… resistance," Randolph explained, finally managing to say the word.

"Please, Randolph," Gadabout pleaded, trying to take the attention away from the boy.

The taller man waved his wand in Gadabout's face. "Shut it! Go on, boy. What resistance? Against whom?"

"Abaddon, sir," Randolph replied, prompting the two men to exchange glances.

"He's just a simple boy with a vivid imagination. Doesn't know what he's talking about. Perhaps you could release him, and we could have this conversation among us, the adults."

"Shut it!" the taller man ordered. "One more word from you, and you'll be sorry. Go on, boy. What else?"

"There's been whispers of a small following, sir, one inspired by a wizard. Some call him the dark wizard, and others call him the shadow. But some say he's the swallow, because of all them paper swallows, them that flies out of his hand, sir."

"Just rumours, you understand," the shorter man chimed in. "And the chattering of a child."

"No, sir, not just rumours," protested the boy, unfazed. "Years ago, I saw him with me own eyes. He saved many children in me village from Abaddon's raiders. A fearsome creature followed him. Like a … big giant enormous wolf! Some say he's evil, but I don't think so.

"Because you don't save children if you're evil, sir. Me mother was killed though, me only family. As for me, I was forced to fight in Abaddon's army but I ran away. Couldn't stomach the killing, sir, so I became a paci … what's the word? A pacifist."

"A what?" asked the shorter man.

"It's a mental condition he has. An exceedingly rare and serious illness," Gadabout injected.

But the boy continued. "I was homeless sir, thought I'd starve. That's when Gadabout found me, gave me food, and kindly offered me a job. He was kind, sir."

The taller man sneered at Gadabout and Randolph. "An escaped convict and a deserter, wandering the land together. What a pair!"

He began to laugh manically, and the shorter man joined in.

Then, the taller man abruptly stopped and adopted a deadly serious expression, but the shorter one continued chuckling.

The taller one elbowed his companion to cease the laughter.

The taller man's command rang out, "Turn around and kneel," as both men pointed their wands at Gadabout and Randolph.

"Do as they say, Randolph," said a flustered Gadabout. Turning and dropping to the ground, Gadabout whispered in a low tone, ensuring the two men behind couldn't overhear, "I can only divert their attention briefly. When I give the signal to run …"

"I'm done me fair share of running," declared Randolph, maintaining his deadpan expression. "Please. I won't run anymore."

Gadabout gave a wry smile, tears welling. "Then I'm sorry," he said gently.

"It's been a pleasure to assist Gadabout the Great, sir," Randolph defiantly declared.

"Tell me about the maiden you fell in love with," Gadabout asked, again deflecting.

"Now, sir?"

"Yes, please," Gadabout replied in a soft tone.

"Well, sir, I had never witnessed such beauty. She worked at that tavern we visited some time ago. She had one blue eye and one green, and a nose with a slight bend. Her breath carried the stink of onions. It reminded me of me mother, sir."

Gadabout awaited the impending blow. Yet the blow didn't come.

Gingerly and at a glacial pace, Gadabout turned around, and Randolph followed suit. Before them loomed a pair of massive, ebony-furred, sinewy legs.

As their gazes ascended, the grotesque sight of a towering and menacing wolf-like creature revealed itself. The shock and astonishment gripped Gadabout and Randolph, leaving them rooted to the spot, unable to divert their eyes from the horrifying spectacle. After an interminable moment of paralyzed silence, it was Randolph who finally found his voice.

"Sir," he began tentatively.

"Yes, Randolph," Gadabout replied.

"This is that monster thing I was talking about, sir."

"And your description was surprisingly precise."

Lord Cecil and Robert suddenly appeared from behind Argog.

"I told you it was the wizard from Naru, from that stage show," Robert remarked to Lord Cecil.

"And so it is," Lord Cecil concurred.

"Ah, fans of my show, I see," Gadabout responded cheerfully, but the trio offered no reaction.

"We are forever in your debt. You saved our lives. If we could be of any use?" Gadabout got up and retrieved his wand and the drawing that had crumpled on the dry, grassy ground.

He carefully tucked it back into his doublet pocket under his long gown.

"No, and it's best you don't tell anyone you saw us, for your own sake," Lord Cecil replied. With that, Lord Cecil, Robert, and Argog began to walk away into the dusky night air.

"Excuse me," Gadabout inquired, scanning the surroundings. He and Randolph hurriedly followed the trio. "What happened to those two charming men?"

"Dead," Argog grunted as they continued walking hastily.

"Perhaps we could be of service to you, then. And it was remarkably fortunate that you happened to be in this exact spot. I would call that fate, a coming together, a destiny, or serendipity, as one might say. We were meant to be good friends," Gadabout suggested.

Lord Cecil abruptly came to a stop, his thoughts lingering in contemplation. "No. It's best you continue on your way," he insisted firmly. The trio briskly departed, leaving Gadabout and Randolph standing in the lingering traces of their presence.

"I'm confident our paths will cross once more," Gadabout declared and waved, his gaze fixed on the disappearing trio shrouded in the veil of the dusty night air.

Chapter Thirteen:
The Blind Old Man

The salty wind lashed across the open landscape, its teeth bared against the approaching dusk.

Alone and terrified, Lily lay prone, peering over a craggy overhang. Below, nestled amidst the sprawling emptiness, stood a quaint thatched cottage. Her attention was soon drawn to an old frail man, a wooden cane in one hand and a bucket in the other. His cane tapped out a steady rhythm, a metronome for his blind pilgrimage alongside the vibrant patchwork of vegetables. His ghostly white eyes, veiled like frosted glass, seemed to stare sightlessly at the soil. He felt the size and texture of each vegetable, carefully selecting the ones deemed worthy for his bucket.

Lily's wand twitched in her grip as she rose cautiously, her steps hesitant as she neared the old man. Startling her, the old man spoke. "I've lived a life unnaturally long," he rasped, a quiet acceptance gracing his words. "I welcome death with open arms, like an old friend. But mark this, young one." His voice lowered, tinged with a sombre warning. "Blood begets only more blood. Yet, you didn't come here to kill me, did you?"

The old man slowly rose to his feet with the aid of his cane.

He turned towards Lily, his terrifying white eyes now in full view. "No need to fear, girl," he reassured her. "I won't harm you." He moved within a few feet of her, and she instinctively stepped back, grasping the wand in her right hand tightly.

He held out his hand, his touch gentle as he reached out to touch her face.

She retracted slightly, unsure whether to trust him. "Don't be afraid, child," he murmured. Lily allowed him to touch her face, his touch conveying a sense of warmth. "Brave, loyal, pure, and rebellious," he whispered, his voice filled with curiosity. His hand moved down, patting her right arm, and feeling at the wand in her hand. "Where is the wizard who gave you this wand?"

Lily paused for a moment, recalling the horror she had just witnessed hours earlier.

"Dead," she replied, her voice barely a whisper.

The old man stepped back, his voice still raspy yet also surprisingly serene. "Are you certain, girl?" he asked as if doubting her words.

"Yes, I'm certain," Lily affirmed, annoyed by his questioning. Her body began to tremble as she clenched her jaw, desperately trying to push the gruesome visions from her mind.

The old man turned away and gingerly picked up the wooden bucket, his movements laboured and slow. He walked towards the cottage, his gait unsteady but determined.

"Questions gnaw at you, girl. And if what you say is true, a nearly impossible task awaits. Yet in impossibility's garden, courage, a lily unfurls, and within resilience, seeds blossom into fragrant possibility," the old man said, his enigmatic voice like smoke in the twilight.

Lily gripped her wand tighter, the smooth wood a comforting anchor against the rising tide of doubt and fear. The flickering embers of the approaching night painted lengthy shadows across the bleak landscape, as if trying to engulf her. Yet, she swallowed her fear, and with a deep breath, followed the old man's fading figure, uncertain of the journey ahead.

Epilogue:
The Rise of Abaddon

The excerpt that follows is a gripping excerpt from Flavius McGinley's acclaimed work, *The Goblin Nation: The Rise of Abaddon 1912*. It weaves a vivid tapestry of Abaddon's formative years, spent amidst the perils of the goblin caves and fuelled by a relentless hunger for power.

McGinley conjures up the hazardous depths of the goblin mines in which toil and cruelty are the currency of survival.

Abaddon's shrouded origins only cast a deeper shadow of intrigue and danger over his tale.

There was once a young and sweet-natured boy who had been brought to the goblin caves as a slave, where he was subjected to the harsh conditions of the dark, cold, and hazardous mines deep underground. His origins were unknown, and the boy was the subject of much debate and rumour amongst the other slaves.

As time went by, it became apparent to those working alongside him that the boy possessed an extraordinary gift, magical abilities beyond his own understanding.

However, he quickly learned to keep his powers hidden, anxious that the goblins overseeing his work would see it as a threat and punish him severely.

A blind, aged man who had been a slave in the mines for as long as anyone could remember became a beacon of hope for the young boy.

Despite his blindness, he knew every nook and cranny of the cave better than any other slave down there. It was whispered amongst the slaves that the blind old man had taken the boy under his wing and –

protected him from the worst of the goblins' brutality. At night, the only time the slaves got to rest, the blind old man would sit with the boy and impart his knowledge.

At great risk to himself, the blind old man secretly taught the boy simple charms and curses, soothsaying, and other frivolous forms of magic of no consequence.

He would recite to the boy classical literature and poetry too, these simple lessons a welcome distraction for the boy from his backbreaking labour and the constant threat of abuse.

The young boy's life was irreversibly altered when the blind old man was brutally assaulted by a pair of goblin sentinels, and his concealed magical abilities surged to the forefront. Consumed by seething anger, he unleashed a formidable burst of energy that swiftly dispatched the guards. He ventured towards a notorious cave, renowned for its colossal opening above that permitted a slender ray of light to infiltrate from the surface via a narrow aperture at its zenith. The aperture was a cruel mockery meant to augment the torment of the enslaved workers, deceiving them with a delusive hope of escaping their predicament. However, not a single slave had ever surmounted the perilous ascent and lived to tell the tale, despite numerous attempts by some who were cognizant of the fatal consequence of their plunge to their doom.

Nonetheless, the boy persisted and began to climb. He emerged from the cavern's aperture, and the sudden inundation of radiant light blinded him momentarily. His joy of escape was fleeting, however, as he was abruptly accosted by _Mida,_ a repulsive goblin.

Mida was a cunning, malevolent, astute, and shrewd creature, with unsurpassed expertise in all magical things. Perceiving a peculiar aura surrounding the enslaved boy, Mida shielded him from retribution and took him under his wing, becoming his surrogate father and mentoring him in the ways of the goblin.

Time passed, and the boy metamorphosed into a prodigious scholar.

Upon reaching maturity, he was christened Abaddon, in accordance with the goblin tradition. He rapidly climbed the ranks, attaining the status of one of the most potent figures in goblin society, and eventually ascending to leadership after his predecessor, goblin Frodekt, challenged him to a magical duel, intimidated by Abaddon's brilliance and ascent to power.

However, Abaddon ruthlessly dispatched Frodekt in the battle. Despite his victory, he had to prove his worth to the other goblins by undertaking the Lurid, an abhorrent and gruelling trial that aimed to test one's fortitude and resilience. The Lurid was a ceremonial test that all goblins aspiring to become leaders had to endure, involving being thrown into an enchanted cave deep within the goblin mines and confronting one's deepest fears. Only those who survived the Lurid were deemed worthy of leadership. Abaddon emerged triumphant from the Lurid, thus cementing his place in goblin society, earning the acceptance and respect from the goblins.

Abaddon's rise to power was not without its challenges.

Some of the goblins were distrustful of him, for he would never be a true goblin. However, Abaddon's strength of character and leadership qualities quickly silenced his critics.

He proved himself to be a master strategist and a skilled politician, always one step ahead of his enemies. With Mida's teachings and his own magical abilities, Abaddon forged alliances with other powerful goblin factions, outmanoeuvring his rivals.

The account by Flavius McGinley encapsulates the essence of this notorious leader. Abaddon rose from meagre beginnings to become one of the most influential figures in goblin society, propelling his people into a new epoch of prosperity and power. Beyond the goblin world, he is widely regarded as one of the most formidable and dreaded wizards of all time.

End of Book 1